Uptown/Downtown in Old Charleston

UPTOWN/
DOWNTOWN
IN OLD CHARLESTON

Sketches *and* Stories

LOUIS D. RUBIN, JR.

The University of South Carolina Press

Published by the University of South Carolina Press
Columbia, South Carolina 29208

www.sc.edu/uscpress

Manufactured in the United States of America

19 18 17 16 15 14 13 12 11 10   10 9 8 7 6 5 4 3 2 1

Library of Congress Cataloging-in-Publication Data

Rubin, Louis Decimus, 1923–
    Uptown/downtown in old Charleston : sketches and stories / Louis D. Rubin, Jr.
    p. cm.
    ISBN 978-1-57003-909-6 (cloth : alk. paper)
    1. Rubin, Louis Decimus, 1923– 2. Jews—South Carolina—Charleston—Biography.
    3. Charleston (S.C.)—Biography. I. Title.
    F279.C49J5788 2010
    975.7'91504924092—dc22
    [B]

                                                                    2009051101

This book was printed on Glatfelter Natures, a recycled paper with 30 percent postconsumer
waste content.

For Eva
I dedicate this book to the Onlie Belovèd,
fifty-eight years after it got under way.

Contents

AUTHOR'S NOTE

The sketches and stories in this book take place in the 1930s and 1940s, mostly in and about the city of Charleston, South Carolina, where I grew up. They were written separately and originally published that way. I have worked them over some, both to cut down on duplication and to make them into a more nearly consecutive narrative.

As anyone who might be familiar with some of my previous books may recognize, not a little of the material is compulsive. That is to say, as memory it has kept forcing itself upon my imagination, as if demanding further exploration.

I would caution, however, that by no means everything in what follows actually took place, and, of what did, not necessarily as described—or even to me. The stories were written as fiction and shaped for literary purposes. The authenticity being aimed at was not that of the recording historian.

What I have sought to do was to be faithful to the time and place as it presented itself to those involved. This has meant trying not to make people aware of what with hindsight they should have been aware of but weren't. Some of what I failed to see when it lay all around me is difficult to credit. I am thinking in particular to matters of civil rights and economics.

The following is a list of the first publication of the stories and sketches that follow. They have been revised, sometimes extensively, for this book.

"Prologue: Adger's Wharf," *Small Craft Advisory: A Book About the Building of a Boat*, Atlantic Monthly Press, 1991.
"The Shores of Tripoli," *Southern Review*, Autumn 1984.
"The Left-Handed Glove: A Memory," *Virginia Quarterly Review*, Spring 1993.

"The Man At the Beach," *Virginia Quarterly Review*, Autumn 1982.

"*Finisterre*," *Southern Review*, Autumn 1978 (repr. *Best American Short Stories*, 1979).

"The Boll Weevil and the Triple Play," *The Boll Weevil and the Triple Play*, Tradd Street Press, 1979.

"A Sort of a Saga" (original title: "The Barreled Sunlight Painters and The Rose Garden Rebels"), *Sewanee Review*, Winter 2002.

"The St. Anthony Chorale," *Southern Review*, October 1980 (repr. *Best Amercan Short Stories*, 1981).

"Epilogue: The Route of the Boll Weevil," *A Memory of Trains: The Boll Weevil and Others*, University of South Carolina Press, 2000.

I am grateful to my longtime fellow conspirator, Shannon Ravenel Purves, for her reading of this manuscript.

L. D. R.
Chapel Hill–Pittsboro, North Carolina
June 2009

Adger's Wharf

When I was a teenager in Charleston, South Carolina, I spent many hours along the Downtown waterfront. In those days, the 1930s and early 1940s, there were not one but two different and seemingly discrete Charlestons. For more than one reason, they could be designated as Uptown and Downtown, and often were.

Downtown Charleston was the old part of the city, with buildings that dated back to colonial times. It was the city that the tourists came to see, and where the "old" Charlestonians lived, the families whose forebears were the antebellum rice planters and merchant princes. Downtown Charleston was a city of narrow, sometimes winding streets with quaint and historical names like Longitude Lane and St. Michael's and Price's and Bedon's and Stoll's and Do As You Choose alleys and Tradd and Church and Water and Gibbes and Legaré and Lamboll and Orange and East Bay. In church affiliations it was Episcopalian and Huguenot and Presbyterian, with a few Unitarians and Congregationalists and Reform Jews whose tenure often went back to colonial and early federal times.

Downtown people were lawyers and doctors and professors and realtors and bankers and stockbrokers and businessmen and artists and writers and newspaper editors. Black people Downtown were "colorful" and "primitive" and wore bandannas and spoke Gullah, and they went about the streets hawking fish and shrimp and produce, and everyone knew their picturesque vending cries. The women wore uniforms to work and had names like Viola and Evalina.

Downtown was steeped in history, and its residents talked about and some few even remembered the firing on Fort Sumter, and Downtown was where there had been pirates and privateers and Revolutionary War heroes and blockade runners and Civil War generals. The older Downtown homes had outbuildings behind them that had once been slave quarters. Downtown there was culture and art, and painters and etchers made illustrations of the famous Sword Gates and St. Michael's Church and the flower ladies on its portico and other quaint scenes, and authors wrote poems and stories and sketches extolling the uniqueness of the Carolina lowcountry, and the Dock Street Theatre performed plays, and there were concerts and recitals. Downtown was the place of the College of Charleston, the nation's oldest municipal college, and the Historical Society and the Library Society and the New England Society, and also the St. Cecilia Society, where the females of the gentry made their entrance into social life.

Downtown was White Point Gardens and the Battery, with Fort Sumter visible across at the harbor mouth, and where the Fort Sumter Hotel and also the Villa Marguerita (which didn't accept Jews as guests) were located. Downtown families were named Alston and Ball and Barnwell and Cheves and Drayton and FitzSimons and Huger and Lowndes and Manigault and Maybank and Mazyck and Pinckney and Porcher and Ravenel and Rhett and Simons (with one *m* only) and Smythe and Stoney and Vanderhorst and Waring; sometimes they even bore several of the names at the same time.

For recreation the Downtown residents kept sailing craft at the Carolina Yacht Basin, and they went sailing off the Battery and held regattas and raced snipes and scows and cruised in handsome yawls and ketches and schooners. They played tennis and golf. They hunted ducks in the abandoned rice fields of the lowcountry. They rode horseback and held fox hunts and steeplechase races. Downtown, in sum, was patrician and cultured and historical and scenic and romantic and literary. When you read about Charleston in a poem or a book it was always Downtown Charleston. If you saw a picture of the city in a magazine or in a painting or watercolor, Downtown Charleston was what was portrayed.

Uptown, by contrast, was plebeian and middle class and ordinary and not at all scenic and cultured and literary. Uptown people were named Bowman and Bierfischer and Blanchard and Bolchoz and Burmester and Castanes and Cohen and Connolly and Condon and Dennis and Finkelstein and Hesse and Jones and Karesh and McLaughlin and Morse and

Muckenfuss and Murphy and Pearlstine and Rosen and Rubin and Shokes and Simmons (with two *m*'s) and Smith (spelled with an *i*, not a *y*) and Thomas and Wineberg. The Uptown streets were straight and not narrow, and bore names such as Maple and Poplar and Cypress and Peachtree and Grove and Line and Bogard and Allen and Cleveland and Alberta and Dunnemann. Uptown there were no lanes and no alleys.

Uptown people were Baptists and Methodists and Lutherans and Catholics and Greeks and Jews. They were storekeepers and carpenters and mechanics and salesmen and policemen and navy yard workers and clerks and certified public accountants and dentists and power company linemen and railroad men and streetcar conductors and bus drivers and branch managers and merchants and pharmacists. The black people who worked Uptown did not wear bandannas and uniforms and did not sell flowers and were not picturesque.

Uptown there was almost nothing historical. There were railroad stations and freight yards and, north of the city limits, a few factories and the navy yard. There was a park with flowers and duck ponds and a zoo, and the campus of the Citadel, the military college of South Carolina, but the park was not old, and the campus was a new one, not the historic Old Citadel of pink buildings with crenellations that was there when the cadets fired on the steamship *Star of the West* at the outbreak of the War Between the States.

There were no old and quaint buildings and gateways Uptown. The houses had front porches, not piazzas, with lawns and gardens fronting the street and in clear view, not in the side yard and back and visible only through ironwork gates. No tourists came from afar to see Uptown Charleston; the guidebooks did not describe its colonial charm. There were no historical societies Uptown, and girls who lived Uptown did not make their debuts.

For recreation Uptown people went to the movies, to baseball games at College Park, and to boxing matches, and they played baseball and basketball and poker. If they had boats, they were powered by gasoline engines, not sails, and were used for fishing. They did not race in regattas. When they played golf it was at the municipal links, not the country club. They were interested in cars, and they did not own horses and go fox hunting. Uptown people did not write or read poems, publish books, or do paintings and etchings. Uptown, in short, was middle class and democratic and every-day and practical, and very, very real.

SOCIALLY THE CITY OF Charleston was a very class-conscious city. As usually happens in such a place, not only the descendants of the pre–Civil War plantation gentry, most of whom lived south of Broad Street, but all the other elements in the population, from the top to the bottom of the social hierarchy, were divided into strata. Each successive stratum aspired to the next higher one on the scale and looked down on the stratum just below it. Another word for this is *snobbery*—and Charleston was a very snobbish place in those days. This was true of the Protestants, the Roman Catholics, the Jews, the Greeks; it was true of the whites and the blacks. One reason for this was that there wasn't much money around Charleston then, and thus only so much opportunity for conspicuous consumption. Inher-ited social position was almost all there was to be snobbish about, so that almost the only area in which persons in search of status could look to demonstrate it was in genealogical distinction.

THE JEWISH COMMUNITY, of which my family was part, was like every-one else divided into Uptown and Downtown. K. K. Beth Elohim, the Downtown, Reform congregation, was the oldest Reform temple in the United States. B'rith Sholom and another synagogue were the Uptown, Orthodox congregations. Although the division was not really geographi-cal, where one resided on the Charleston peninsula tended to reflect the degree of each group's assimilation into the local secular culture. (The sub-urbs, of course, were another matter.)

The Reform congregation was made up of what remained of the old Sephardic Jewish families of colonial and early federal days, the German Jewish families of the mid– and late nineteenth century, and some latecom-ers. The Orthodox congregations were mostly of relatively more recent advent—Russians and Eastern Europeans who held on more closely to the customs, traditions, and language of the preimmigrant past.

Reform services were in English. Certain responses were written in Hebrew in the prayer book, but few members of the congregation could read them. There was a choir and organ music and no cantor. The dietary laws were observed, if at all, in very lax fashion. In short the Jewish community was undergoing the same process of assimilation that had gone on and was still going on within every American immigrant group from the early 1800s onward. Because Charleston was a small city, lacking enough people within the various ethnicities to constitute themselves into permanent enclaves, the assimilative process could be relatively rapid.

When I look back and try to make sense of what was involved, certain things strike me. The Downtown, Reform congregation, to which my family belonged, was very small; there were only three people in our confirmation class at Sabbath school. The congregation had dwindled away over the years, as people moved away or intermarried. In truth it was a dying community and in certain respects no longer displayed a distinctive ethnic identity at all.

The result was that by the time of my own generation—the generation growing up in the 1920s and 1930s—those who remained held on self-consciously to their position, looked down socially upon the Orthodox community, and took satisfaction in their supposed absence of secular identity. Judaism, they told themselves, was not an ethnic matter, but purely religious and theological (this while across the Atlantic the Nazis were making no such distinction).

Snobbery always involves pretense of course. The person who places a premium upon social status is almost always trying to prove something— not only to others but oneself. My own family for example did not extend back lengthy generations into Charleston life; my grandfather was European born—and in East Prussia or Lithuania, not western Europe—and came to the city only in the 1880s. Yet, for reasons that are not still quite clear to me, we were unquestionably part of the Downtown congregation. As I look back, I realize the extent to which my generation imbibed this way of thinking and feeling from infancy onward. In effect we were raised and tutored in a snobbery that was all the more absurd for being so specious.

IN MY OWN INSTANCE, the result was that I inhabited two worlds when I was growing up and was not wholly or fully of either, the more so because my literary ambitions and my interest in music and history were largely solitary activities. In my imagination, as someone who would some day become a writer, the Uptown and Downtown that I knew were discrete entities, linked by the slender umbilical cord of the Rutledge Avenue trolley and later bus line that as a high-school and college student I rode from our house at the edge of the northern city limits to the Downtown city on the lower peninsula.

That, I have come to believe, is in no small degree where Adger's Wharf and my lifelong fascination with boats—and particularly workboats—comes in. Part of their lure for me, and that of the Cooper River waterfront in general, lay in the unique fusion, geographical, psychological, and cultural, of the two Charlestons that they offered to my imagination.

The small craft berthed at Adger's Wharf were shrimp trawlers, cargo launches that served the nearby Sea Island communities, commercial fishing boats, the harbor pilot boats, crab and oyster buyboats, and a variety of other small craft. At the head of the south wharf were the three tugs of the White Stack Towboat Company. At the base of the north wharf was a large, mostly open-sided shed with a wide galvanized tin roof, where the catches of the shrimping fleet were bought, sorted by an array of black women, iced down, and shipped out. Just upstream and abutting Adger's Wharf was a boatyard with a marine railway and a machine shop. The area was always busy.

Adger's Wharf was considered to be one of the tourist attractions of the city; the trawlers and launches were frequently extolled in magazine articles as contributing to the "quaintness" and the "romantic atmosphere" of an old seaport town. By the mid-1930s, when I grew old enough to spend time down on the waterfront, make-and-break gasoline engines had replaced the sail power of the once-numerous "mosquito fleet" that seined for shrimp outside the harbor.

Before the advent of good roads, and bridges linking the Sea Islands to the mainland up and down the South Carolina coast, water transport had provided the principal means for moving passengers and goods between the city of Charleston and the farms, plantations, and small communities along the coast. Adger's Wharf, at the foot of Tradd Street, was where many of the small shallow-draft launches in the island trade had docked.

By my time these had mostly succumbed to competition from automobile and buses. The trawlers and other workboats that did tie up at Adger's Wharf tended to be motley affairs, many of them owned by black fishermen and painted with garish colors and odd decorations, including more than one "eye" to ward off the evil spirits lurking in the deep.

With their nets hung out to dry, their trawl boards and donkey engines, and the pungent aroma of dead fish and shrimp spoiling in the hot sun, these workboats were picturesque enough, I suppose. So were the Lock-wood tugboats with their tall white stacks topped in black, from which wisps of smoke always trailed as their engines were kept ready for duty. And so too were the numerous sea gulls that constantly dipped and soared overhead, in wait for whatever might materialize in the way of discarded fish, shrimp, or other organic refuse in the water about the wharf.

Yet *I* certainly did not think of Adger's Wharf and its inhabitants as scenic, picturesque, colorful, or anything of the sort. The boats I saw there were mostly workboats—designed for commercial duties on the water—and if there was considerable glamour about them for me, it was in their sturdy, practical quality, just as the Seaboard Railway trestle downstream from our house, or the freighters and tugboats that passed by on the Ashley River, were fascinating to watch.

The sailing craft at the Carolina Yacht Club, downstream from Adger's Wharf, held little interest for me, nor did I feel any desire to go over to the foot of Calhoun Street on the other side of town and look at the sailboats and power yachts berthed at the new yacht basin on the Ashley River. There was something artificial about these boats. The working craft at Adger's Wharf, and the docks and wharves along the Cooper River from there northward, were what held my attention.

A short distance farther upstream were the Clyde-Mallory Line docks, three large, green-painted enclosed wharves where the passenger ships that operated between New York City and various South Atlantic and Gulf Coast ports came in from the ocean to discharge and take on passengers and freight. Except for one ship, the *Henry R. Mallory,* the Clyde Line ships bore Indian names—the *Shawnee,* the *Iroquois,* the *Seminole,* the *Cherokee,* the *Algonquin.*

They were all small ships as passenger liners went, designed for coastal service. In New York Harbor, where the great transatlantic liners were regular callers, they would doubtless have been considered insignificant affairs indeed; but to a youth who had never seen the likes of the *Berengaria, Aquitania, Mauretania, Bremen, Ile de France, Queen Mary, Normandie,* or any of the other oceanic greyhounds, the coastal liners seemed enormous.

The Clyde liner that I saw most often was the *Cherokee,* a single-stacked ship that berthed along the outside wharf when it called at the docks and so was visible from the shore. It was there every Saturday morning, and it departed in midafternoon. Once when I was six years old and we were spending the summer out on Sullivan's Island across the harbor, my father had gone to New York City on business and was returning aboard the *Algonquin*. The harbor channel led close to the island, and very early in the morning my mother had taken us down to the beach to see it come by. It was a gray dawn and misty. My father tipped a deckhand to let him blink a ship's lantern at us from the deck. Thereafter the *Algonquin* was my ship. Some day in the future, I told myself, I would travel aboard it to New York.

I was never to achieve my ambition, for when World War II broke out, all coastwise passenger service was suspended and not afterwards resumed. I sometimes wondered what had become of those little ships. Once I was returning aboard the *Constitution* from a summer of lecturing in southern France, and out on the stern one evening I struck up a conversation with a black crewman who it turned out had worked aboard the Clyde-Mallory ships during the 1930s.

The *Cherokee*, he told me, met a disastrous end. Its cabins and super-structure were constructed of plywood, he said, and during the war, pressed into duty with the navy, it was torpedoed by a U-boat off Nova Scotia. The flimsy superstructure crumpled, and the ship went down within a matter of minutes. As for the *Algonquin*, it had eventually been sold to a Turkish shipping firm, and as far as he knew, it was still in service somewhere in the Black Sea.

TO THE NORTH OF THE CLYDE-MALLORY DOCKS, at the foot of Market Street and behind the stately U.S. Custom House, were also numerous small craft, as well as the old Cooper River Ferry terminal. In the 1920s, before the immense twin-spanned Cooper River bridge was built across Charleston Harbor from the town of Mount Pleasant on the eastern shore, a pair of sizeable ferryboats, the *Palmetto* and the *Lawrence*, traversed the bay. The latter had tall smokestacks and a large walking beam atop the cabin; the *Palmetto* was a diesel-powered craft without such conspicuous trappings. Years later I was struck by a description in William Styron's novel *Set This House on Fire* of the ferryboats that during his childhood had traveled between Newport News and Norfolk, Virginia: "those low-slung smoke-belching tubs which had always possessed their own incomparable dumpy glamour." For there *was* a glamour about such craft, box-like and double ended, so perfectly adapted to their function.

To drive aboard en route to the beach was an exciting business, the family car clumping down the serrated steel gangway between the huge clusters of pilings ringed at the top, onto the deck and along a narrow avenue to our assigned parking place. Then the rattle of the chains in the sprocket-wheel hoist mechanisms as the gangway was drawn up free of the deck, and the throbbing rumble of the engines and the rocking motion beneath the deck as the ferry moved out from the slip and into the harbor. Usually we got out of the automobile and went up a stairway to the upper deck, to sit on wooden benches and watch as the ferry made its way across the bay.

Midway across, the two ferries passed each other, engines churning away, intent upon their missions. Then, as the wharf drew near and we returned to our automobile, came the abrupt cessation of the engines' steady pulsation as they disengaged their gears. The ferry glided silently dockward, only to have the engines roar into action again, this time in reverse, as the forward momentum was stemmed. The wide bow of the slowed boat bumped along the pilings, slipped by them as they swayed back, then came to a stop in front of the wharf. Then more rattling of chains as the ramp was lowered, the protective guard chains were removed, and one by one the waiting automobiles jounced across the gangway and up the ramp into the terminal.

By the time I was able to visit the waterfront on my own, the *Palmetto* and the *Lawrence* had been out of service for half-a-dozen years, the new Cooper River Bridge having usurped their clientele. The only ferry still in operation from the terminal behind the Custom House during the 1930s was a small, open-decked affair operated by a Captain Baitery, which, powered by a single diesel engine, plied the waters between Charleston and Sullivan's Island, requiring an hour's transit time each way. From the shoreline I watched the boat creep across the harbor past Castle Pinckney, its engine droning a low, thin monotone. Still, it was a working ferryboat and worthy of its own dignity.

The docks farther up the river were where the freighters put in. Their masts and cargo booms were visible above the roofs of the warehouses, unapproachable behind high chain-link fences. Not so the small, white-hulled steamships of the United Fruit Company's Great White Fleet; their operations were open to view from the land. Standing at the foot of the wharf, I could watch the stalks of green bananas coming ashore on roller ladders in a steady stream, to be grasped by black laborers and borne toward the yellow open-doored railroad refrigerator cars. Outside the entrance to the wharf, strings of railroad cars were shunted into position.

Strung out all along the shore of the waterfront were the rusty-railed tracks of the Port Utilities Commission, linking the various wharves with the outside world and with sidings leading to warehouses Downtown. Occasionally a locomotive would be working these tracks, a small, grimy switcher with standing boards in front for the brakemen to ride upon as the locomotive spotted some boxcars and collected others. The flanged steel wheels squealed as curves were being negotiated, the locomotive emitting considerable smoke and much noise as it came and went.

FROM ADGER'S WHARF to the ferryboat dock behind the Custom House was my territory. I knew it all, every step of it, every pier and piling. Most of all, however, it was Adger's Wharf itself that drew me like a magnet. On Saturday mornings I would linger there for hours at a time watching the proceedings, waiting for the tugboats to cast off their lines and go over to the Clyde Line dock to help the *Cherokee,* now bedecked with pennants, extricate itself and back out into the channel, then swing its bow downstream and proceed southward under its own power, very slowly at first, past Adger's Wharf and the High Battery until it turned toward the mouth of the harbor.

Eventually the ship was no more than a long low shape in the water out beyond Fort Sumter, bound for New York or Jacksonville. But by then it was getting toward late afternoon and time for me to walk up Broad Street to Meeting Street. There at the post office I boarded the Rutledge Avenue car that would take me all the way uptown to Sans Souci Street and home.

IT WOULD BE MANY YEARS before I would begin to understand why Adger's Wharf had such significance for me. One reason I was so drawn to the Charleston waterfront—its ships and cargo launches and tugboats and trawlers—was that it seemed to fuse two otherwise discrete realms of my experience. It was the stuff of literature and the imagination and yet was *not* self-consciously picturesque or quaint but immediate and real and important to me. The workboats *belonged* on the Downtown scene, as that scene figured in my experience; yet they were Uptown in function, in appearance, and in the identity of those who worked aboard them.

Workboats didn't sail in regattas, or go cruising along the High Battery with the fashionable people aboard. Rather they carried freight and pulled barges and trawled for shrimp. But they did those things out on the waterfront, out in the very harbor where the pirate ships had once sailed, and the British bombardment of Fort Moultrie had taken place, and the Confederate guns had opened fire upon Fort Sumter.

NOWADAYS ADGER'S WHARF is gone from the Charleston waterfront, as are the Clyde Line wharves that were next to it. The area has been made into a park. The ship channel no longer runs along the Downtown waterfront. Today's seagoing vessels enter the harbor and depart over beyond Castle Pinckney. To see the shrimp trawlers and other such workboats one must drive over to Shem Creek, across the harbor. Not only are the ferryboats gone, but the lofty, cantilevered steel bridge that succeeded them has been replaced by an even more massive, imposing span. It is only in my memory that the city of sixty-two thousand inhabitants, bordered on the north by Mount Pleasant Street and on the south, east, and west by water, divided into an Uptown and Downtown of which I was part of both and of neither, still exists.

Yet my imagination still inhabits the place as it was in 1930s and early 1940s; and what the intervening years have done is not to change the city that my memory knows, but only the distance from which I view it.

| 1 |

THE SHORES OF TRIPOLI

When I think of the events drawn upon to make this story, it is as though there were a wall dividing everything coming before and afterward into separate kinds of existence. A better image than that might be a tunnel, a railroad tunnel, whereby one watches from a coach window as a train is moving along on a sunny day, viewing the scenery, and then an abrupt plunge into darkness. For as long as it lasts nothing is visible other than momentary forms, flares of light, on and on, a seemingly unending extension of shape and sound. Then just as suddenly it is daylight again, and distance, and beyond the tunnel the excursion proceeds on its way, but with a changed configuration.

ALMOST SINCE I COULD remember we had lived on Hampton Park Terrace, though I did have some recollection of an apartment Downtown. Our house was on President Street, and I was in the second grade and walked seven blocks to school each weekday morning and back in the afternoon. We had a backyard with a swing set just like those in the park and also a pyramidal tent and a sandbox and a garage, which was never used for our car. I knew everybody on the block on both sides of the street, and the park was only two blocks away.

When I heard about the new house Downtown, I did not particularly like the idea of moving to it. My father explained that now that my little brother was learning to walk and no longer slept in a crib, the house on President Street was too small for us. "You and Edwin will have a great big room, with your bed on one side and Edwin's on the other," my father said. "You'll have space for your electric train and your soldiers right there on the floor. It's a nice big house. You'll like it."

My brother was big enough to get around now without crawling. He could talk too, though sometimes he didn't get the words exactly right. My sister was too young to go to school yet.

I was the oldest. "You must set an example," my mother told me.

We were going to move into the new house in January, as soon as the people who now lived there moved out. On our Sunday afternoon drive we went by Bennett Street on our way home and saw the house. It was large and painted light yellow and white, with a big front porch, and instead of a garage there was a roof extending from one side of the house, with the driveway leading underneath. Next door was a large vacant lot, and across Gadsden Street from the lot was the lumber mill. "You'll be able to watch the boats bring in logs from the river," my father said. "They'll keep them in the mill pond."

I would be going to a new school, Bennett School. My father had gone there when he was a boy, he said, and also my Uncle Edward, who had won the Bennett Medal when he graduated. I asked my uncle about it, and he showed me the medal, which he wore on a watch chain. It was made of gold. Perhaps when I got to the seventh grade and graduated I would win the Bennett Medal too, my aunt said. That would be nice, though I thought I would prefer the kind of medal that soldiers had, with a ribbon that you could pin on your chest. My father had that kind of medal from when he was in the United States Marines during the world war. There was a picture of my father in his uniform, with his rifle on his shoulder, standing guard at Camp Paoli. That was before I was born.

One of the good things about moving to the new house would be that it was only a few blocks from Uncle Edward's house. Uncle Edward had not been in the war, but he knew all kinds of tricks and songs and games, and every Sunday morning, when my father's porter, Sam, took us Downtown to visit him, he had a present for me and my sister. There was another uncle, named Ben, who lived up in New York City and wrote plays. Uncle Ben had not only been in the war, but he had been wounded in a battle called the Argonne Forest. When he was in town he played soldier with me. We were in no-man's-land on patrol, and suddenly Uncle Ben would whisper "Freeze!" because there was a star shell. "Freeze" meant to stay still and not move a muscle, because if you did the Germans would know you were there and open fire. When my uncle said "Freeze!" I felt shivers run through me, even though it was not that kind of freeze.

If you were a soldier, you had to be brave. My uncle had been a lieutenant in the army. When I grew up I was going to be a United States Marine like my father. If you were in the marines you sang "From the Halls of Montezuma" when you marched.

Another thing that was good about the new house was that in the backyard there was a wide lawn, which my father said would be good to practice golf shots. On my last birthday, he had brought me a golf bag and a set of clubs, not little toy clubs but real ones cut down to my size. I played golf with them in the backyard now, but the yard on President Street was small and there was no grass. The yard in the new house was much larger and had grass, and I would be able to practice my chip shots, my father said.

On one Sunday in January, only a few days before we were to move Downtown, my father did not go to play golf as usual. He was sick, and my mother kept the bedroom door closed and did not let us come in to see him. Late that morning the doctor came. In the afternoon, instead of going for a drive, my sister and I were taken out to the park by our nurse, Rosa. It was chilly in the park, and when we went to feed the ducks, the water in the lake looked very cold. I wondered whether there would be any ducks to feed in the lumber-mill pond across from the new house.

We stayed out in the park until it was almost dark, and when we returned home, it was Rosa who gave us supper, because my mother was busy taking care of my father. At bedtime my mother came in and heard my prayers. I did not fall sleep right away but lay in the dark for a long time listening to a noise that sounded like someone was calling. I wanted to ask my mother what it was, but I had promised her to be quiet and not wake Edwin. So I sang "From the Halls of Montezuma" in a low voice and pretended I was in no-man's-land, and the lieutenant said "Freeze!" and I lay very still without moving a muscle for as long as I could.

After a while I heard a freight train blowing across the river and listened as it came across the Seaboard trestle and into the city, along the tracks beyond Hampton Park. The sound of the rolling train wheels drowned out the calling noise. It was a comforting sound.

When I woke up the next morning I had a memory of hearing some voices during the night and Rosa coming into the room and telling me to go back to sleep—which was strange too, because she was never there at night.

I dressed myself and went out into the hall. The door to my mother and father's room was open, and I looked inside. The bed was made, and there was a blanket folded at the foot, pale green and pasty looking. The room was dark and everything in it seemed gray. The brown paneling in the hallway looked heavy and frowning. My brother and sister were still asleep, and everything was quiet. I could hear Rosa and Florence talking downstairs in the kitchen. I went into the bathroom and brushed my teeth and then went down to breakfast.

"Your daddy's gone to the hospital," Rosa said, "and your mama's gone there with him."

"How long is he going to stay at the hospital?"

"I don't know. Your momma said to tell you you got to be the man of the house while your daddy is sick."

That afternoon when school let out I walked home as fast as I could, to see whether my father had come back from the hospital. Instead, my Aunt Marian, who lived in Augusta, Georgia, was there to stay with us. She was waiting on the front porch with my sister. When I asked about my father, Aunt Marian said it would probably be several weeks before he came home.

"Is he having his tonsils out?" my sister asked. Once my sister and I had gone to the hospital to have our tonsils taken out and had stayed for two nights.

"No," Aunt Marian said, "he has an abscess in his ear. He's gone to the hospital so that they can make it stop hurting."

That was what the calling noise must have been that I had heard last night. "What hospital is he in?" I asked.

"He's at St. Francis Xavier." St. Francis Xavier was where we had gone to have our tonsils out, and where my brother had been born. It was a Catholic hospital, and the nurses were called sisters and wore blue gowns and large white hats that looked like sails.

"Are we going to see him?" my sister asked.

"Not right away. When he's feeling better," my aunt said. "Now let's go and ask Florence to serve dinner."

It was odd to be eating dinner with only my sister and Aunt Marian at the table. My father always came home from his store for dinner every afternoon at two o'clock.

Edwin began to cry upstairs. Though he was too little to eat at the table with them, my mother always brought him down and let him sit in the high chair and eat an apple. Today my mother was not there, and Rosa had not remembered to go and get him. I heard Rosa going up the steps, and after a minute Edwin stopped crying. She brought Edwin down and placed him in the high chair.

"Appoli," my brother said. "Me appoli."

"Edwin wants an apple," I told Rosa.

Rosa returned with the apple and gave it to my brother. I wondered whether Edwin understood that my father was in the hospital.

My mother came home that evening just before it was time for me to go to bed. "Your daddy is very sick," she told me before she heard my prayers, "and he won't be ready to come home from the hospital for several weeks."

"Does it hurt him?" I asked.

"Not now. They've given him some medicine for it. On Friday we're going to move to the new house," she said, "and I want you to be good and do your best to help Aunt Marian to take care of Jean and Edwin, because you're the oldest and have to be the man of the house until your daddy's well again."

"Why don't we wait to move until then?"

"Because our lease on this house runs out and the new tenants want to move in on Monday. When your daddy comes home, we're going to be all moved into the new house, and we'll surprise him."

During the next several days almost everything in the house was packed up. My mother was at the hospital during the day, but my father's porter, Sam, and the nurse and cook were busy putting things into boxes and rolling up rugs and taking down pictures and curtains.

Each afternoon Rosa took my sister and me out to the park. The house seemed very empty, with some of the boxes already gone to the new house and with the walls bare and no curtains on the windows. Thursday afternoon my aunt and I put my toys and books into boxes. I kept out the book that my father had studied in the United States Marines during the war, which had drawings of soldiers marching and presenting arms and firing rifles.

That night, after my mother had come home and heard my prayers and turned out the light and gone downstairs, I stayed awake for a long time.

With the rugs gone from the floors I could hear whenever anyone moved about downstairs. I heard the telephone ring, and my mother's voice as she talked on it. Although I could not make out most of what she was saying, I heard the word "operation" several times. An operation was when the doctor did something to you at the hospital to make you feel better. One of my friends at school had had an operation on his appendix, and when he came back to school, he had a bandage on his stomach.

I heard the freight train moving along the tracks on the far side of the park. This is my last night in this house, I thought. It would be strange to go to bed tomorrow night in a new room. I waited for sleep to come, thinking about the new house and how surprised my father would be when he came home from the hospital and we would be all moved in. As soon as we got there I was going to take my golf clubs out into the yard and begin practicing my chip shots, so that when my father came home I would be able to show him how well I could play.

To make a chip shot you used a niblick, and the ball was supposed to go up into the air and come down near the hole. I had a golf ball that had a knitted cover, so that I could swing hard at it without the ball flying too far. When I grew up I was going to be the new Bobby Jones, my father told me, and win the grand slam. I also had a set of real boxing gloves, and sometimes my father boxed with me. My father got down on his knees and said, "Put up your dukes!"—which was what boxers said before they fought. Once when we were boxing, I slipped, and my head hit against my father and made some blood come on his chin. My mother told us to stop, but my father only laughed and wiped the blood off with a handkerchief. "It's just a scratch," he said. "Don't worry about it."

When you got in a real fight you did not use boxing gloves. A boy on the next block had fought me one day at school. I had been afraid to walk home down Huger Street, and had gone over to Congress Street and had taken a long time to get home. When my father came home from the office I told him, and my father said for me to tell the boy that he would not buy gasoline from his father anymore.

My mother said that my father would not come home for several weeks. Several weeks could be two weeks, couldn't it? Two weeks seemed like a long time to wait, though it depended on how you thought about it. Once my father was due home on the train from New York City, and we were going down to the station to meet him. I was ready to go an hour ahead of time, and I waited in the living room until it was time to go, and it had seemed that the hour would never go by. But if you were doing something else, an hour did not take nearly as long.

Every night the big clock on the mantel downstairs struck four times, a little song, and when an hour came, it rang the little song four times and then once for each o'clock. But tonight the clock was packed up to go. Tomorrow night at the new house I hoped it would be back on the mantel again, so that I could hear it.

When I left for school in the morning a large yellow moving van was in the driveway and movers were carrying the furniture from the living room down the front steps and into it. Aunt Marian was going to meet me after school and take me to the new house. I felt excited.

This is the last time I will be walking to school along Huger Street, I thought. The first day I had gone to school I had been afraid, but I liked it now. My teacher was Miss Annie Turtletaub, who was a friend of my father and mother and had come to our house for dinner on my birthday. The classroom had green blackboards, and along the top of them was a long strip of paper with the letters of the alphabet, big *A* and little *a* and so on. At first I was in the slow reading circle, but now I was in the fast circle, and each day we read in the *Elson Reader*. I wondered whether I would be in the fast reading circle at Bennett School.

When it was time for us to have our writing lesson, Miss Turtletaub said she had an announcement to make. She told the class that I was moving away and that this was my last day with them. She said that my father was sick and in the hospital, and she wanted everyone in the class to write a letter to my father asking him to get well. On the blackboard she wrote my father's name, and then everybody wrote letters.

I did not know whether to begin my letter like that or to write *Dear Daddy*. Miss Turtletaub told me to write *Dear Daddy* on mine. I wrote "Dear Daddy, please get well soon so we can play golf at the new house. Love, your son." When they were done Miss Turtletaub collected the letters and put them into a big envelope. Then they sang "For he's a jolly good fellow which nobody can deny." Then the bell rang and school was over.

Miss Turtletaub gave the envelopes with the letters to me to hold, and took me to the principal's office, which was where you had to go when you were bad, but not this time. I had gotten dirty playing horseback fighting at recess, so Miss Turtletaub washed my face and my knees. My aunt was waiting for me in the office. Miss Turtletaub walked to the door with us and kissed me, and I felt very sad.

Outside on King Street, Sam was waiting for us in my father's car. As we drove downtown my aunt looked at the letters and said that they were very nice and would make my father feel better when he was able to read them. We drove down Rutledge Avenue to Calhoun Street. Creticos Fruit Store was on the corner. I was about to tell my aunt that Creticos was where we always stopped after our Sunday drive to buy fruit for supper, when I saw that we were driving past St. Francis Xavier Hospital. I looked at the white concrete building and the screened porches along the side. I wondered which window was the one to my father's room.

THE FIRST NIGHT THAT I slept in the new house I woke up in the middle of the night. I had been dreaming about playing in Hampton Park and going over to the monkey cage at the zoo there to see Pete, an old monkey who did not look like the others but had shaggy black fur and usually stayed by himself on a perch at the back of the cage. In the dream the other monkeys had begun throwing wood chips at Pete, and the keeper had come and chased the other monkeys away, and Pete had jumped on the keeper's shoulder and begun screaming. I woke up then and looked around to make sure I was not really in Hampton Park but in my room. At first I expected it to be my old room, and then I remembered that I was now in the new house with my brother asleep in the bed across the room.

It was only a dream, I told myself, and lay in the darkness. I felt a little afraid even so, and I wanted to call to my mother, but when I went to bed she had told me to be sure not to wake up Edwin. I could hear the Seaboard freight train crossing the trestle, but in the new house it sounded far off in the distance. After a little while the clock rang, and I went back to sleep.

IT TOOK A LITTLE TIME to get used to the new house. The furniture and rugs and pictures and everything else were the same, but in their new places they looked different. I took my golf clubs out into the backyard on the grass, to practice my chip shots with the knitted golf ball, but I hit the ball up on the top of the toolshed, and Rosa said I would have to wait until Sam came over on Sunday morning to get it down.

The lot next to the house was overgrown with weeds, and in one place I found some old bones. I wondered whether they had been left there when the earthquake had come, before I was born. My aunt had told me about the earthquake, and said that buildings had caved in and some people had been killed and injured.

Across the street from the vacant lot was the lumber-mill pond. I crossed over and looked at it. There were logs floating in the water. At one end there was a gate in the water with some long rusty chains attached to it. There were no ducks. I picked up some pieces of oyster shell from the sidewalk and began throwing them at a stick floating in the water, pretending that I was a United States Marine firing at a German battleship.

After a while my aunt called for me to come back home and asked me not to go over to the mill pond by myself. I felt sure that my father would not be afraid to let me go, but I would have to do what my aunt asked until my father came home.

Monday morning my aunt took me to Bennett School. As we were crossing Ashley Avenue I looked up past the palmetto trees and oleander bushes along the sidewalk two blocks away and could see the corner of the hospital.

We walked on past the Charleston Museum, then down Rutledge Avenue to Bull Street. When we crossed Pitt Street, Aunt Marian said, "Do you know that we used to live right down this street once?"

"Did I live there too?"

"Oh, that was long before you were born. Your father hadn't even met your mother back then."

"Was Daddy a little boy like me when you lived here?"

"No, he was older by then. When he was your age we lived on St. Philip Street, just up the street from Bennett School."

It was further to walk to Bennett School than to the old school. We walked past the College of Charleston campus and turned into St. Philip to the doorway to the school. Inside the hall was dark, and the ceiling was very low. Bennett School seemed much older than James Simons School. We entered a room marked "Office," and Aunt Marian told the lady at the desk that we were here to enroll me in the second grade. The lady led us into another office, where a man with a fat stomach and a double chin was seated at a desk. He stood up and shook hands with my aunt. "This is Mr. Strohecker," my aunt told me. She explained that my father was ill and in the hospital.

"Yes, I know that," Mr. Strohecker said. "Too bad, too bad." He had a deep voice. He put his arm around my shoulder. "My boy," he told me, "if you can be as good a student as your father was, you will do very well."

Mr. Strohecker asked my aunt some questions, and wrote on a piece of paper. Then he called to the lady at the desk. "Take this young man to Miss Riley's class, please," he told her.

"I'll be back for you about one fifteen," Aunt Marian said to me.

The lady took me down the hall, along another corridor, and opened a door. We went into a classroom, and all the boys and girls in the room turned around and stared at me. I felt very nervous, and wanted to go back to my aunt, but the teacher came and shook my hand and asked me what my name was, and then she introduced me to the other pupils and led me to a desk next to a window at the end of the front row.

They were doing their arithmetic, so I got my Vireo tablet and pencil box out of my book bag, and watched as the teacher wrote numbers on the blackboard. The room was smaller than the room at the old school, and instead of windows all along the wall, there were only three windows, and the electric lights were turned on overhead. I watched out of the window at the schoolyard and at the cars passing by. When my father was my age, he lived right down on the street. It was only a block from King Street, where my father's store was located.

When he was well again I would be able to walk over to the store after school. I could go into the radio-repair room and watch Mr. Lunney and Mr. Forrest Greer fixing radios, and they always put a pair of earphones over my head and let me listen.

I looked around and saw that everyone was looking at me. The teacher had stopped talking. She must have asked me a question.

"I didn't hear," I said.

"I'm sure you didn't. How much is five minus three?"

"Five take away three is two."

"Very well. Now you must pay attention to the lesson, not to the automobiles on St. Philip Street." Everyone laughed.

AFTER RECESS WE READ in a book about General Lee, and how in the midst of battle he saw a little baby bird fallen out of its nest, and how General Lee got off his horse and lifted the bird back up to its mother. The teacher told us to draw a picture of General Lee and the bird, and I drew one. She looked at it. "Very good," she told me, and held it up for the class to see.

The next day I walked to school by myself, and when school was out I walked home with two boys named Gordon and Fricky, who said they lived on Halsey Street. Fricky's father had a sailboat, and took him sailing out in Charleston Harbor all the way past Fort Sumter. I told about how my father took me to Savannah on the train, and we stayed in a hotel, and from the window I could look down at the river, which was yellow from the mud.

We reached the corner of Rutledge Avenue and Bennett Street, and Gordon and Fricky turned into it. I was about to go with them. Then I had an idea.

"I've got to go to the store," I said. I crossed Bennett Street and walked past the front of the museum and under the trees along the oyster-shell pathway to the artesian fountain on the corner of Calhoun Street. I looked up Calhoun Street to where St. Francis Xavier Hospital was in view a block away. I crossed the street, and walked down to the hospital. The front door was on Ashley Avenue.

My heart was beating very fast. For a moment I waited, and then I walked up to the door and into the hospital. The hallway was lined with potted palms along the sides. Down the hall I could see a desk, with a nurse seated behind it.

I was about to go up and ask her where my father's room was, when a door opened close to where I was standing, and a nurse stepped out. I looked inside. Several men dressed in white and with round white hats were standing next to a big table. There was a huge light overhead, and the men were wearing gloves, and had little white masks over their noses and mouths. On the table was a man with his head on a pillow and a white sheet over him. One of the men had a red spot on the front of his white uniform.

I walked back to the entrance door of the hospital as fast as I could. As soon as I reached the sidewalk outside I began to run. I ran to the corner, and across Ashley Avenue, and across Calhoun Street, and along Ashley Avenue all the way to Halsey Street, before I stopped to catch my breath. That was blood on the sheet, I thought. My face was very hot, and I was sweating, but even so I was shaking inside, and my legs felt weak.

I waited for my heart to stop pounding in my chest. I was lucky that my mother did not know what I had done. My insides were still shivering, and

I felt very strange. It was like when my uncle whispered "Freeze!" so that the Germans would not see me in no-man's-land.

That wasn't my father they were operating on, I told myself. At least I know that.

Wishing to seem brave, I began to sing as I walked on to the new house:

From the halls of Montezuma
To the shores of Tripoli. . . .

2

RIDDLE ME THIS

A Trio of Incidents

In what follows I want to tell about three incidents. They took place in the early and middle 1930s. During those years, our family moved nine times. The process began when I was seven years old and continued until I was almost twelve and beginning the seventh grade of elementary school. There was one school year when I changed schools four times.

Each time I was escorted to a new school and introduced to a new teacher. As I entered the classroom and was assigned to a desk, I could sense the eyes of the boys and girls in the class staring at the new boy. At recess time I wandered through the schoolyard, watching everyone playing and talking, knowing nobody there. When school was done, I walked home by myself, until after a few days I began to make some friends.

This was during the years of the Great Depression of the early 1930s. My father, an electrical contractor and merchant, had come down with a brain abscess from which he was several years in recovering. I had a dim memory of having heard groans coming from his closed bedroom door late one evening and the next morning discovering that he had been taken to the hospital, first in Charleston and then another in Richmond, Virginia, where my grandparents and my mother's brothers and sisters lived. Several times he had been expected to die, though I did not know it at the time, and for months afterward his head was wrapped in bandages. By the time we moved back to Charleston, his once-thriving business was in desperate shape, and he was forced to declare bankruptcy. Thereafter much had changed.

The second-story flat into which we moved was less spacious than our previous home. As it turned out, we were to live there for more than two years. We were not in want, though neither were we wealthy.

Unlike the fathers of my playmates, mine no longer went to the office each day. Before taking sick he had been active in business and civic affairs, but he had been warned by his physicians not to try to return to work, either for himself or as an employee; the nervous strain and financial anxiety might well prove fatal. After a time his physical condition improved, and he no longer wore bandages or walked with a cane. He was not fully recovered, however, and indeed was never to be entirely free of the effects of his illness. The enforced leisure soon grew heavy on his hands. He had never been much of a reader, nor did he have hobbies. For the first time in his adult life, he found himself bored and discontented, with no escape in sight.

Despite my parents' efforts to keep the full impact of what was happening from their three children, I was aware of the emotional tension in what was going on. There was one night when I woke up late at night to hear him coming along the hall, and the thought crossed my mind that perhaps he might murder the family and commit suicide. I can only suppose that I must have read in the newspaper of some such event having taken place somewhere. For so bizarre a notion to have come to a ten- or eleven-year-old child, it seems obvious that I must have sensed his frustration and unhappiness.

IN THE NEW NEIGHBORHOOD, on Rutledge Avenue just south of Broad Street near Colonial Lake, there were numerous children my own age. The Baker boys, Ronald and Markham, lived next door, and next to them the Hairston brothers, Charlie and Johnny. Across Rutledge Avenue were the Jerveys, the Joneses, and the Ostendorffs. The Stellings lived further up the block, and several houses down from us were the Pinkussohns. All of us were enrolled in Crafts Elementary School, which was five blocks away, and in the afternoons we usually played together.

On weekends our routines diverged. Together with the Pinkussohn children, my sister and I attended religious school at the Reform Jewish temple on Saturday mornings. The other families on the block, none of whom was Jewish, all went to church on Sundays.

When Sabbath school was done I walked up King Street to the Majestic Theater to see a movie and the latest chapter of the current serial. The feature film was always a western starring gunslingers such as Ken Maynard,

Colonel Tim McCoy, Bob Steele, Hoot Gibson, and Johnny Mack Brown. This was before the vogue of the singing cowboy, and none of the two-fisted, hard-riding rustler-busters we admired would have so demeaned himself as to break into song.

Another, more prestigious tier of cowboy stars did not have their oat-manship exhibited at the Majestic. Films in which Tom Mix, Buck Jones, Hopalong Cassidy, and George O'Brien appeared were shown on Monday and Tuesday afternoons at the Garden Theater, a more elegant movie house. To see a movie there on the afternoon of a school day required special parental dispensation.

It was a western movie that was the occasion for the first of the incidents that I want to tell about. Word had arrived that a new Tom Mix movie was coming to the Garden Theater the next week. The Hairston brothers, whose parents were liberal in authorizing activities on school afternoons, were planning to see it. Ronald and Markham Baker reported that they too would be going.

I introduced the subject of the Tom Mix movie at dinnertime, but permission—or of equal importance an offer of wherewithal—was not forthcoming. The day following, however, I was presented with a quarter by my uncle, and was able to persuade my mother to sanction my attendance at the Tom Mix movie in company with the others.

On Monday afternoon we pedaled over to King Street, chained our bicycles to the fence in the parking lot behind the theater, bought our tickets, and went inside.

Of the movie itself I have no recollection. When it was over and we emerged from the theater, we were caught up in the excitement of Tom Mix's exploits, and there was much shouting, shooting, and staggering from the impact of bullets from six-shooters.

It was while we were unchaining our bicycles that we became conscious of an odd sound. It seemed to be coming from the second-story window of a building immediately above us. A man was singing, though to no tune or rhythm that I could identify. It was a male voice, drawn out, the notes and pitch rising and falling, sounding more like a wail than a song. Or was it singing at all?

We looked at each other. As we mounted our bicycles, Markham Baker began to yodel in response: "O-lee-O-lady-O! O-lee-O-lady-O!"

"O-lee-O-lady-O!" someone else yodeled back.

"O-lee-O-lady-O! Turn off your ra-di-o!" By the time we pedaled out of the driveway and onto George Street, everyone was yodeling back and forth. Everyone except myself.

We were soon beyond earshot of the parking lot, but the thought of the seemingly tuneless singing, if that was what it had been, remained with me. As I rode along on my bicycle, I felt gloomy, apprehensive.

At supper that evening I described what I had heard. "Was it behind the Gloria Theater?" my mother asked. When I said it was, she explained that the sound must have been coming from the Jewish Community Center on St. Philip Street, the rear windows of which overlooked the parking lot. A cantor must have been practicing his chant, she said.

Not only had I not encountered a cantor's chanting before then, but I was unaware of the existence of a Jewish Community Center. I knew very well, of course, that there were Orthodox as well as Reform Jews, and that when we had lived Uptown several of my playmates had attended something known as *shul*, were not allowed to eat ham, and received presents not for Christmas but from someone known as the Hanukkah Man.

What we had heard, my mother said, was a recitation of prayers in Hebrew, half singing, half intoning. When Orthodox boys became thirteen years old, they prepared for a bar mitzvah, at which they joined the rabbi on the altar, read aloud from the scriptures in Hebrew, and sang or chanted prayers, also in Hebrew. Someone was probably being taught by a cantor, my mother said.

"Why don't we ever do that at our temple?" I asked.

"Because Reform Jews don't believe in chanting. We have an organ and a choir."

In retrospect what is most intriguing about the incident was my reaction to it. I seem to have recognized, or else intuited, something about the sound that caused my response to differ from that of my companions. So far as I know, I had never been taken to an Orthodox Jewish synagogue or heard a cantor in action; yet I seemed have picked up the Jewish overtones and in doing so been reminded of my separateness from my companions.

THE SECOND INCIDENT ALSO happened during those years and belongs in this account. In the summer we spent much of the time beneath the Bakers' house, which was set well back from the street and elevated above the ground. White beach sand had been spread over an area. We had toy soldiers, cars, trucks, and other things, and we built a town in the sand. The Bakers' cousin Pauline, who was younger than Ronald and Markham, came over sometimes to play with them. So did another girl, Peggy Magwood, as on occasion did my sister, although she generally preferred the company of two older girls who lived down the block.

That summer—it must certainly have been in 1934—the Chicago World's Fair was in the news. The newspapers, magazines, and newsreels were filled with its doings. Widespread attention was devoted to Judy Garland, Sally Rand, and other associated events. The streamlined railroad trains, the Burlington Zephyr and the Union Pacific City of Salina, were much written about.

Ronald Baker owned an electric jigsaw, and we shaped some wooden pieces to resemble the locomotives and coaches. We smoothed off a rail bed in the sand, improvised grade crossings, signals, a viaduct, stations, a roundhouse, and train yard.

One afternoon when I went next door, Ronald and Markham Baker were already at work down under the house, as were the Hairston brothers and Buddy Ostendorff. After a time Peggy Magwood came over and announced that a special performance from the world's fair was about to begin. We followed her to an area closed off on three sides. which had sometimes been used as a stage. Across the open side a length of clothesline was strung, with an old bedspread fastened to it with clothespins. A wooden plank had been set before it atop cinder blocks for seats.

Peggy Magwood disappeared behind the curtain. After a minute she emerged. "Ladies and gentlemen!" she announced, "presenting Sally Rand and her world-famous fan dance!"

She pulled back the curtain. Pauline Baker was standing on the stage toward the rear in semidarkness, partly wrapped in an army blanket. She stepped forward and began to dance, swinging the blanket back and forth, at intervals holding it entirely away from her. She was totally naked.

For a half minute her performance continued, with appropriate gestures and movements. Then she retreated back into the full shadow at the rear of the stage.

"That's all," said Peggy Magwood. "The show is over!" and began refastening the curtain to the clothesline.

Nothing was said. Nobody applauded. We got up from the bench and went back to where we had been playing in the sand.

The next morning I was at work on the train station under the Bakers' house. After a while Ronald came down. He reported that Pauline's parents had found out about his cousin's performance, and she had been punished.

"They called my parents about it," he said. "My mother says it was very bad to show herself to boys. Especially to you."

"Why?"

"Because you're a Jew."

I said nothing and continued to work on the train station.

IT WAS APPROXIMATELY A YEAR later that our family moved once again, for what would prove to be the final time during my childhood, although of course I did not know that at the time. By then I was eleven years old, and our new house was located far uptown near the northwest corner of the Charleston city limits, on a bluff overlooking the Ashley River. There were two neighbors close by and otherwise only open fields, salt marsh, a tidal creek, and, along the river's edge, stands of water oaks for a half mile to the east and a mile northward and to the south.

We moved in as soon as classes were over for the school year. The new house, financed with the help of a government-guaranteed loan, was built both to provide more living space and, at least as importantly, to give my father something to occupy his attention. In this it certainly succeeded because thereafter gardening, planting fruit trees, and otherwise cultivating and improving almost an acre of land kept him quite busy.

It was on a Sunday afternoon the following May, when I was twelve years old, that the third incident took place. I was invited to a bar mitzvah party for the son of a friend of my parents whose family were Orthodox Jews. It was to be held at the Jewish Community Center. By that time I had become more aware of religious and social distinctions and assumptions.

On the appointed afternoon I rode downtown with my parents and my brother and sister. I was to be dropped off at the party, and when it was over, I would return home on the streetcar. There was considerable traffic backed up on St. Philip Street, so when we were a block away I got out of the car and walked down the remaining half block and up the stone steps to the entrance. Inside people were standing about, adults as well as girls and boys my age or older, talking and laughing. I looked around, but saw no one that I knew.

Suddenly I turned and stepped back out through the doorway. Down the street our car had not yet reached the stoplight at the corner of St. Philip and George streets.

I raced down the stairs to the sidewalk, still clutching the bar mitzvah present I had brought, sprinted across the street through the traffic and along the block, pulled open the door of our car, and flung myself into the backseat. I commenced to weep hysterically. I did not know why.

"It's all right," my mother assured me, leaning over the seat back and patting my head. "You don't have to go to the party if you don't want to. We'll send Stanley his present tomorrow." The traffic light changed, and my father drove on. The entire episode could have taken no more than several minutes. Some time elapsed, however, before I could make myself stop weeping.

IN LATER YEARS, thinking back over the incident, I tried to understand what it was that had caused my sudden bolting from the reception. Up to the moment that I had entered the crowded room I had felt no conscious anxiety. It was by no means the first time that I had been invited to a party. Why then did I feel such panic?

Obviously the location of the reception must have had something to do with it. It was from the open windows of the Jewish Community Center above the theater parking lot that several years earlier the strange singing had come that my mother had explained was the chanting of a cantor. Until then I had not known of the existence of the center, which in those days was sponsored almost solely by the two local Orthodox congregations. In both instances, as the child of Reform Jewish parents and taught to consider myself as set apart from less assimilated Jews, I was being made to confront my Jewish identity.

In the same way the episode of the Baker's girl cousin dancing naked under the Bakers' house had been a reminder that whatever I had been taught to the contrary, in the eyes of our neighbors the fact that I was a Jew set me apart from my playmates. Why was it that I had reacted as I did to Ronald Baker's comment about my presence at his girl cousin's performance in the nude? Obviously he been told that by his parents.

All three episodes, therefore, had to do with Jewishness, and in each instance my youthful response had been a manifestation of Jewish anti-Semitism, which in those years was an all-too-common attitude among Reform Jews.

There was more involved in than that, however, as I later came to realize. In reply to Ronald Baker's remark I had said nothing. Instead of being angered, I had been embarrassed. Was that not because I had felt guilty at having witnessed what I had seen—and would have felt so even if no religious or social overtones had been involved?

As for the bar mitzvah party, that event was essentially a puberty ritual, a social occasion designed to celebrate a youth's formal admission into the adult congregation. Upon entering the room I had confronted the gazes of persons I did not know, including girls and boys my own age and older and grown-up men and women. Once again my role was that of being made to face a roomful of strangers—and with the additional implications of emerging adolescence. The sudden glimpse of what lay inescapably ahead had prompted my flight.

IN THE YEARS THAT FOLLOWED I would go over in my mind the emotions involved in these incidents. The linkage between them became more evident to me, and I understood some of the reasons why the details persisted in my memory. Yet there was one aspect of the riddle that would continue to perplex me for years to come. It had to do with the earliest of the three episodes.

It will be recalled that, instead of being amused by the singsong chanting that we heard after seeing the Tom Mix movie, as my companions had been, I had felt disturbed and apprehensive. At supper that evening my mother had identified the sound as that of a cantor singing at the adjacent Jewish Community Center.

The obvious explanation for my response was that was the unexpected chanting had served to remind me, as the lone Jew among my playmates, of my anomalous status. This even though, at the time it happened, I had not attended an Orthodox Jewish service or heard a cantor chanting and did not know that there was a Jewish Community Center, much less that Orthodox Jewish boys were taught to chant in Hebrew at it.

Still I ask myself this. Even granted that it must have been because somewhere, somehow, I had previously heard a cantor or rabbi singing in Hebrew, would that of itself have been a sufficient explanation for its impact upon me? I had felt not merely embarrassed or uncomfortable, but depressed, and even apprehensive, as if I had reason to dread what the chanting was suggesting.

Over the years the memory of the experience recurred, an unsolved riddle that was not so much important as simply perplexing. It would not be until I started to think about writing this story that an answer began to suggest itself.

The voice that I had heard had seemed to rise and fall, not exactly tuneless but to no regular cadence, almost like a wail. It had been an adult male voice, as if a lament, or even the moan of someone in pain. This was not long after we had moved Downtown, within less than a year after our return from Richmond, when I had been ten years old.

When before had I heard a male voice, rising and falling, as if groaning in pain? And what had been the consequences, for me, for my family?

Riddle me this.

3

THE MAN AT THE BEACH

From the top of the Ferris wheel at Folly Beach, you could see a long distance in all directions, up the beach to where it was woodland along the shore and beyond that the black and white rings of the Morris Island lighthouse tower, northward to the flat marshland beyond the wide creek that separated Folly from James Island, and to the south the ocean, green-blue to the far-out horizon, beyond which lay nothing but water all the way to the coast of Africa. It was almost like being in an airplane, except that there was the steel grid of the giant wheel that, though it revolved, was anchored firmly to the earth.

The amusement park was across the way from the pavilion. We headed for it as soon as my father parked the car. Uncle Leo's car was right behind, and Maynard and Elaine hurried across to join us. Uncle Leo and Aunt Sophie were not really our uncle and aunt, but we had always called them that. There were five children in all—Maynard and Elaine, my sister and my brother, and myself. Maynard, at thirteen, was the oldest, and my brother, who was seven, the youngest. Each of us had money for three rides and an ice cream cone when done. My brother always went straight for the merry-go-round. There was one horse that was his favorite, painted red with a silver mane and saddle. He climbed aboard it, grasped the reins securely, and would use all three of his tickets one after the other.

What I liked were the electric cars. There were several dozen of them, and when the current was turned on, they all glided around the circle. The cars had metal rods that thrust up from the cockpit like the mast on a sailboat, and as the rod atop them made contact with the electric grid there were continual flashes and sparks and a strong odor of ozone, much like the atmosphere of a thunderstorm. The cars had thick rubber bumpers and steered very loosely, and the trick was to bump into one car and sent it spinning into the path of another. But if you were not careful, and sometimes even if you were, someone was apt to run into your car, and before you knew it you were caught in the melee, frantically turning the steering wheel while your car slid sideways out of control.

Maynard and I got into one car. My idea was to move to the outside of the circle and stay out of trouble, but Maynard saw an opportunity to ram into the side of the car bearing my sister and Elaine, and we steered toward it, only to be bumped from behind, pushed sideways directly across their path, and promptly sent flying again. My sister and Elaine were laughing at us, but then someone rammed into their car and off they went too. When the cars stopped moving and the ride was over, my sister proposed that we switch places. She would ride with Maynard, and Elaine with me. So we changed over, and Maynard and I dueled with each other, bouncing against each other's cars again and again as we made the circle, while the girls shrieked and laughed. Finally Maynard's car sent ours sliding halfway across the track and we spun round, until finally I gained control and was about to return the favor, when the flow of electrical current ceased, and the cars slowed to a halt.

On we went to the Ferris wheel, and as the open gondola rocked back and forth we went rising up, seated four abreast, over, down, then up again, until at the very zenith of an orbit the Ferris wheel stopped and, suspended in the air and swaying slowly, we hung in space for a long minute, gazing at the ocean, the beach, the land. A bank of cloud was over the sky to the west. There was a freighter far out at sea, so far that we could see only the superstructure above the horizon. It seemed to be without a hull, only a white cabin and masts and a stack with a smudge of smoke. The Morris Island lighthouse was clearly in view. Then the Ferris wheel resumed its revolution, and we dropped downward, until we could see only the tip of the lighthouse tower, and in a moment it too was completely out of sight.

We walked over to the pavilion, bought our ice cream, then went down to the beach. Our parents were seated in folding chairs beneath striped beach umbrellas. Uncle Leo had on his bathing suit. My father never went swimming. Before his illness he had been a strong swimmer and used to venture far out beyond the breakers, but though he had mostly recovered from the operation on his head he was forbidden to go into the ocean for fear of ear infection. He and my mother and Aunt Sophie sat in the beach chairs watching us as, running ahead of Uncle Leo, we sprinted for the surf.

We stepped out, dodging the incoming waves, until the water was up to our waist. Though it was a very hot July afternoon, the ocean seemed chilly at first, but after a moment we became used to it and settled down into the water with only our heads above the surface. Uncle Leo, however, continued out toward the breakers, striding out to an oncoming comber, then diving through the wall of the rising water as it broke over his head, to emerge well beyond it. Maynard, who could swim very well too, followed him out. I could not swim at all, and I stayed with my sister and Elaine, my head above the water, letting the current sweep around me, occasionally pushing myself up to let the swell of an incoming wave surge past. My brother, as I saw when I looked shoreward, was seated in water up to his waist in a gully at the edge of the ocean's margin. I waved to my father and mother and Aunt Sophie, and my mother waved back.

After a while Uncle Leo went back onto the beach. The four of us stayed in the surf, with everyone swimming around except myself. What I did was to move about, my body outstretched so that my hands were just touching the bottom, buoyed by the salt water, pretending to myself that I was a ferryboat, traveling back and forth, pausing occasionally to dock, and repeating under my breath the bells and whistle signals, just as Tom Sawyer did with the *Big Missouri*. It was enjoyable to push myself about in the surging water, giving way as the waves swept around me but always keeping a hand, or sometimes just an extended finger or two, in touch with the coarse sand of the submerged beach, gently but firmly maintaining my way even as my legs and my body swayed in the ebb and flow.

Later we left the water and went back up onto the beach. My little brother stayed on in the gully. He seemed to be trying to splash minnows into a pool he had dug. When we reached the place where our parents were seated, we saw that a man was standing there talking to them. He was wearing white duck trousers with rust stains on them and a yellow polo shirt and was blond headed. His face somewhat red though his skin was deeply tanned. The man was doing most of the talking, with my father and Uncle Leo nodding and occasionally responding, "Oh, yeah?" and "Is that right?" The man seemed to telling about a voyage or airplane trip or something that he had been involved in and was going into considerable detail, though I could not tell exactly what it was he was saying.

"That your boy?" the man asked Uncle Leo, pointing to me.

"No," Uncle Leo replied, "that's my son over there," with a gesture toward Maynard, who was standing off to the side.

"Going to show you a trick, son," the man said to me. He came over to where I stood, lay down on his back in the sand, and held his arms out in front of him. "Now you run and jump right into my hands, and I'll flip you over and you'll come right down on your feet."

I looked at him. I was not sure just what it was that he wanted me to do, and not especially eager to try it.

"Don't worry," he said. "Just run straight to me, and throw yourself right at my hands. I'll catch you. It won't hurt."

I looked at my father. I stepped back a little way, and ran, not too fast, toward the man, half throwing myself, half falling upon him. He had to lower his hands to catch me, but he grasped me about the waist, and I felt myself being lifted and tossed up and over, so that my legs went over my body and head and I came down on my feet a foot or so beyond the man's head, having executed a somersault in the air.

"How's that?" the man asked. He looked at Maynard. "You want to try it now?"

Maynard nodded. He came running toward the man, launched himself in a swan dive toward the man's arms, and was taken up and tossed in a fly-ing somersault, head over heels, landing upright several yards beyond.

"That's the way!" the man said. "Just run hard and throw yourself at me. I'll do the rest." Still lying with his back on the sand, he turned his face to me. "Now you come try it again. Run hard."

This time I came at him faster, and dived toward him. Once again, but more smoothly, I felt myself being taken in his strong hands and tossed up and over, into the air, and some distance beyond him. As I did I again smelled a strong, raw odor, not exactly unpleasant but quite sharp. It must be whiskey, I thought.

"Can't I try it?" my sister asked.

"I think you'd better not," my mother said.

"I won't let her fall," the man promised.

"Can't I?" my sister repeated.

"Do you think it's all right?" my mother asked my father.

"I think so," he replied.

"Very well, but be careful," my mother told my sister.

Now it was my sister's turn to go sailing above and beyond the man. Then Elaine tried it, and then we took turns, one after the other, somersaulting in the air. The man did not seem to tire. My little brother, who had come over to watch, decided he wanted a turn, and because of his lightness the man flipped him far into the air and he came down, squealing with delight, well beyond where any of us had landed.

"Now, that's enough!" my mother called. "You'll wear the poor man out."

"That's all right," the man told her. "I'm doing fine." He sat up. "Here," he said, this time to Maynard, "let me show you another one. Come here and just stand right over my chest." He lay on his back again. Maynard went up, placed his feet on either side of the man's torso, and the man put a hand around each of Maynard's shins and raised him straight up in the air, over his head. "How's that?" he asked as he held Maynard several feet above him, firmly and without seeming to strain at all. Then the man tossed him deftly sideways and up, and he came safely down on his feet.

"My turn!" my little brother said. Each of us followed. The man's hands were very firm in their grip, and I had no difficulty at all holding my balance, though when he tossed me away I stumbled as I landed and fell to my knees before I could regain my equilibrium.

"You're real strong, mister," my little brother said.

"I'm all right," the man said, grinning at my parents and Aunt Sophie and Uncle Leo. "You're pretty strong, too, I bet."

"Uh huh." My brother flexed his biceps determinedly. The adults laughed.

"That's enough acrobatics for now," Aunt Sophie said.

"Were you really a pilot?" Maynard asked the man. Maynard knew everything about airplanes and pilots. He had books about them, and built balsa models that were highly exact in detail. When he grew up, he said, he wanted to be an airplane designer.

"Sure am," the man said, making a change in tense. "Flew in the Dole Pineapple Derby, Seattle to Honolulu. Finished third, right behind Martin Jensen."

"How come you didn't win?" my sister asked.

"Cracked cylinder head about four hundred miles out. Slowed us down and we finished out of the money. We were ahead till it happened. Flew a hundred feet above the ocean most of the way. Had only five gallons of gas left when we landed."

"What kind of plane did you have?" Maynard asked.

"Beechcraft 17R. Got a picture of it in my bedroom."

"Do you still have it?" my sister asked.

The man shook his head. "Sold it the next summer, when we went barnstorming in Mexico." He pronounced it as if it was spelled *Mehico.* "Too heavy for that."

"What kind of plane do you have now?" Maynard asked.

"Don't have one right now." The man turned to our parents. "How about if I take these kids up to the pavilion and buy them an ice cream cone?"

"That's awfully nice of you," my mother said, "but they've already had some ice cream, and we've really got to be going home." She and Aunt Sophie rose to their feet. Uncle Leo and my father took down the beach umbrellas and began folding the canvas chairs and towels.

"Where did you go in Mexico?" I asked the man.

"Mexico City, Guadalajara, Tampico, Chihuahua—everywhere. Ran out of gas a hundred miles east of Chihuahua, had to land in a cornfield. Nearest gas was fifty miles away. Had to pay a man to go get it by horse and wagon. Spent three days waiting there till he got it and brought it back. Had to live on frijoles and cornmeal. Got sick from drinking the well water, was in the hospital in El Paso for a month."

"Come on, Maynard," Uncle Leo called. "We've got to get going. It's going to rain before long." There were dark clouds coming into view now over the dunes to the northwest.

We said goodbye, but the man came along with us. He began talking to my father. "How about doing me a favor on your way back home? Turn right just past Mazo's and go two blocks. My place is right there. Little white house, all by itself. You can't miss it. How about stopping by and telling my wife I'll be home later?"

"Well, uh, we're sort of in a hurry," my father said.

"Won't take you but a minute. Sure would appreciate it. I got some business at the pavilion. My wife'll be real worried about me."

"Well—," my father said.

"Just go right in, and make yourself at home. There's an ice chest with fresh milk and soft drinks under the cot in the hall. Just help yourself. Take the kids in too. Got pictures of airplanes on the walls."

"We won't go in," my mother said. "We'll just leave word if your wife is home. Come on," she told me. "Let's be going."

"Have you got any pictures from the Pineapple Derby?" I asked.

"Got a picture of me wearing one of them leis," the man said. "Put them around our heads soon as we landed." Then to our parents: "Go right in the house, make yourself comfortable." He turned to me. "You go in and see the pictures. Next summer when you boys and girls come back over here I'll take you for a ride. Take you all over the island, and over to Charleston, and out over the ocean. Won't charge you a thing. You folks, too," he added, addressing the adults. "I'll have my license back next May."

"That's very nice of you," Aunt Sophie said. "Come on, Maynard. We've got to go."

"So long now," the man said. "You just come over and ask for me at Moffett Field, right off the highway a mile the other side of the bridge. That's where I'll be. I'll have my license back," he said again.

The man went on into the pavilion while we walked toward the automobiles, carrying the umbrellas and the chairs. Though the sun was still shining, a bank of dark clouds was rising toward mid-sky, in the shape of a giant anvil.

"How about that?" I said to Maynard. "A real pilot. He was in the Pineapple Derby."

"The book I've got says that the Dole Pineapple Derby only had two planes to finish," Maynard said. "All the others were lost at sea."

"Maybe he got mixed up with another race." Maynard was probably right; he knew all those things by heart.

"He said he flew in a Beechcraft," Maynard added. "The Pineapple Derby was back in 1927, and they didn't start making Beechcraft planes until a couple of years ago."

"He probably just got his dates mixed up," I insisted. "If he was making it up, how come he's got pictures?"

"He was a mite loaded, wasn't he?" Uncle Leo remarked to my father as we reached the automobiles.

"To the gunwales." My father agreed. "He was feeling no pain whatever."

"Do you suppose he really does have a house on the back road?" Aunt Sophie asked.

"We can find out," my mother said. "It won't hurt to deliver his message, I suppose." She turned to us. "Be sure you brush all the sand off before you get in the car."

"Come on, get in," Uncle Leo said to Maynard and Elaine. "If we're going to stop by his house we'd better get moving. We'll be caught in the rain if we don't." By now the sun was hidden behind the edge of a mass of gray clouds. It was hot, and the air felt sticky. I thought I could hear a rumble of thunder off in the distance, though it might have been an airplane.

We drove off. The cars had been sitting in the sun all afternoon long with the windows closed and were very hot. Past Mazo's Grocery we turned right and headed down a sandy road with crushed shell spread along the ruts.

"Are we going to go in his house?" my sister asked my parents.

"No, we'll just deliver the message," my mother said.

"I'd like to see the picture of the plane," I said.

We drove past pine trees and some houses, until we came to a small bungalow with white asbestos shingling, off by itself and with stands of pine trees on either side. There was an old bicycle near the front door, and alongside the house a couple of washtubs and several rusted forty-gallon barrels.

My father stopped the car, and we stepped out. Uncle Leo pulled up behind us and got out of his car. "I'll go see if anyone's home," he said. We stood together in front of the house. I could hear the thunder growling off to the west. The sky was getting dark.

Uncle Leo walked up to the front door and knocked. He waited. No one came to the door.

"Nobody seems to be home," he said.

"Let's go look," said my mother. Uncle Leo knocked again. After a moment he tried the front door handle, and it opened. "Anyone home?" he called. There was no answer. He closed the door.

My mother went up to the door and opened it again. She peered inside. "I don't see anyone," she announced.

"Maybe we ought to leave a note," Aunt Sophie suggested.

"No, there's no use in that," Uncle Leo told her.

"Can I go in and see the airplane pictures?" I asked.

"No," my father said. "You stay right here."

"But he told us to. He wanted us to go in and see the pictures."

"You just stay outside."

We were standing in front of the house with my mother peering through the open doorway, when a woman appeared from around the side of the house with a little girl.

Quickly my mother stepped back from the door. "Your husband asked us to stop by and tell you he was going to be late," she said to the woman.

The woman said nothing. She was small, with light hair, and dressed in a faded green blouse and a pair of yellow slacks. She wore sandals, and her toenails were painted pink.

"He said he had business at the pavilion," my mother explained.

I looked at the little girl. She seemed to be about eight years old, and with long blonde hair and blue eyes. Her face was almost expressionless; her eyes gazed at us. They must have been around back, I thought.

I had the feeling, which grew on me, that no matter how plausible our reasons for having come, we were intruders. There was a blanched look to the little girl and to her mother as well, which seemed to go along with the fading colors of the clothes they wore and the chalky siding of the house, as if the weather had bleached them all to a neutral tone. The girl and her mother stood there impassively while around them the afternoon was growing dark with the thunderclouds that now entirely covered the sun. The air was oppressively thick, and the imminent approach of the storm gave a forsaken cast to yard, house, and inhabitants.

I took it all in—the weatherworn look of the small house, the coming storm, the absence of the man at the beach, the presence of the woman and little girl waiting for him to come home—as with a terrible dreariness. Why did what I now saw appear so wretched?

We must seem like part of the coming storm to the girl, I thought: a group of strange people suddenly materialized at her front door. We were violators.

I felt that if there were in fact photographs of airplanes, then actually to see them would only confirm the dreariness.

"WELL, LET'S GO," my father said after a moment. We returned to the automobiles and got in. I looked back and saw the woman and little girl still standing there watching us.

As we drove off down the road, the wind began gusting strongly, and the sand swirled about us. Then the rain came. It came in torrents, driving at the car windows as we turned into the highway, sweeping across the road. All about us the thunder boomed, and the lightning flashed. My father drove very slowly, peering through the windshield as the wiper blade beat back and forth to clear a narrow field of vision through the streaming water.

"She didn't even say thank you," my mother remarked after a minute. My father, concentrating his attention on the road ahead, made no comment.

"Is that man going to take us for a ride in his airplane?" my little brother asked.

"No, he was just talking," my mother said.

"He was real strong," my brother said. "He threw me way up in the air."

"I smelled whiskey on his breath," my sister said.

The car windows were fogging up. I made an open spot with my hand and looked out at the salt marsh alongside the highway. After a while the storm began to slacken in ferocity, though the rain was still falling steadily. The marsh, which in sunlight was sharp and brightly defined, seemed blurred and diffuse. I tried to make out the shape of the lighthouse tower, which usually was visible in the distance across the marsh, but the rain and haze were too thick. Through the back window, I could see Uncle Leo's car coming along behind us, headlights burning. He too was driving carefully through the downpour, keeping well to the rear.

"Why do you think he lost his pilot's license, Daddy?" I asked.

"I don't know," my father said.

"How do you know he did?" my mother asked.

"He said he was going to get it back next May," I told her, "so he must have lost it."

"Maybe it was because he tried to fly when he was drunk," my sister proposed.

"I don't think so," I said. "He'd have more sense than to do that."

"Well he was drinking plenty today," my sister insisted, "because I could smell it on his breath."

"He wasn't drunk, though," I said. "Was he, Mother?"

"It depends on what you mean by drunk," my mother said. "I think he was just feeling good."

"Maybe he wasn't a pilot at all," my sister said. "He might have been pretending."

"I bet he was!" I declared. "He couldn't have just made all that up. Could he, Daddy?"

"I don't know," my father replied.

"What difference does it make?" my mother said. "It's really none of our affair."

"I bet he *was* a pilot!" I insisted.

"I bet he wasn't," my sister said.

"Oh, shut up!" I told her.

"That will do," my father said. "I don't want to hear any more about it."

I thought of how Maynard and I had steered the little electric cars around the metal floor at the amusement park and had tried to ram into each other's car while Elaine and my sister had laughed and shrieked each time the rubber fenders collided and the cars were jolted from their paths, while the sparks flashed overhead.

The rain continued to fall, and my father drove carefully. Occasionally an automobile would come along in the opposite direction, materializing abruptly out of the downpour with headlights turned on for visibility, and pass by in a rush. The thunder seemed further away now, and there were no more flashes of lightning.

Soon the darkness lifted a little, and it was possible to see objects off in the distance. My father kept his eyes on the road.

4

THE LEFT-HANDED GLOVE

The move into the new house at the edge of the Ashley River meant a considerable adjustment in the way I spent my time. Downtown there had been a half-dozen children my own age living on our block and various schoolmates within walking distance. Now there were open fields, thickets, groves of trees, creeks to the north, east, and south, and the salt marsh and the river to the west.

It was early June when we moved in. School was out for the summer, and the baseball season was in full swing. I was left-handed, and what I lacked and needed was a left-handed glove, to be worn on the right hand. Until then it had not mattered so much. Downtown we had occasionally played softball in the vacant lot across the street but no more than that, and playing baseball was not an important part of my life. Uptown, however, it was by all odds the favorite sport.

It was not that I had been uninterested in baseball before the move. Almost from the time I was able to read the sports pages, I had followed the major league teams in the newspapers. I had never been within several hundred miles of the Polo Grounds in New York City, but I identified my fortunes with the New York Giants and their star left-handed pitcher, Carl Hubbell. Very few of my Downtown schoolmates had seemed to share my interest; even as it grew in intensity, it had remained solitary and intellectual.

By contrast most of the Uptown boys had favorite teams and players and held decided opinions on who would win the pennants and meet in the World Series. They played baseball and talked about it—their own games, the Municipal League games at College Park next to the playground, and the major league games. I wanted to play baseball too, not just read and talk about it.

If I had the proper kind of glove I could ride my bicycle over to Hampton Park playground, a mile or so away, or to Hampton Park Terrace, where I had once lived and knew a few boys, and play baseball there. But the gloves and mitts at Woolworth and Kress were all meant for right-handed boys. Only at sporting goods and hardware stores were left-handed gloves on sale, and these were well beyond my price range. Even the least expensive J. C. Higgins models at Sears, Roebuck began at three dollars.

An appeal to my mother for the funds to buy a left-handed glove would get nowhere, as I knew very well, though I tried it anyway. "You've already got a baseball glove," my mother informed me. "You don't need another one."

"It's not a glove, it's a catcher's mitt. And it's for right-handed players."

"Well, you'll just have to make do with it for now," she declared. "Maybe for your birthday." My birthday was in late November, long after the baseball season would be over.

My father made no comment. Such matters were considered to be in my mother's jurisdiction, and he was uninterested in baseball or other forms of sports. Before his illness he had played golf on weekends but no longer. His health had improved to the extent that he could work in the garden all morning and, after two o'clock dinner and a nap, for the remainder of the afternoon. However, the new house and garden kept him fully occupied—which was what it was intended to do and why the house was built. So my cause was foredoomed.

THERE CAME A WEEKDAY in midsummer when my father drove downtown to purchase something from a hardware store on upper King Street, and I went along with him. While he was conducting his business I looked around the store. On the sporting goods counter I came upon a baseball glove, a junior model, made of tanned leather and with rawhide webbing, on display in a blue pasteboard box. A left-handed glove!

It was priced at only $1.25. I lifted it out of the box and tried it on. It fit perfectly over my right hand. Somehow I persuaded my father to advance the money to pay for it.

On the drive home I was in a state of exhilaration. Again and again I kept removing the left-handed glove from the blue box, pounding my left fist in its pocket. This was no dime-store affair, but a genuine baseball glove, with the cloth label "Hutch" stitched onto the strap. I would be able to field line drives and fly balls, or, as appropriate to a left-hander, even play first base.

As we neared home my father must have noted my excitement. "I don't think I'd say anything about it to your mother right away," he advised.

Alas, my elation over the left-handed glove was more than I could suppress. At dinner I placed the blue carton with the glove out of sight under my chair at the table, but its very proximity was irresistible. It was not long until the left-handed glove was out of its blue box and on my lap.

Upon catching sight of it, my mother's response was prompt. The glove was confiscated. Pleas, promises were to no avail. I had no right to such a thing until I had saved up the money to buy it. There would be no triumphal bicycle ride over to Hampton Park Terrace that afternoon to display the left-handed glove and demonstrate my ability to take a full-fledged part in a baseball game. There was no joy in Mudville. I was desolated.

In actuality the impoundment lasted only for several days. Tasks were found for me to do, and one way or another the money was made available to enable the left-handed glove to be legitimately restored to my possession. Thereafter I missed no opportunity to take part in any pickup baseball games I could find in the area. By the time that the baseball season began yielding to football, I had made some ball-playing friends and renewed acquaintance with others.

WHEN SCHOOL OPENED in September, it was my third stay at the James Simons Elementary School, and this time I did not have the uncomfortable sense that I was once again the new boy, up for inspection by a classroom of strangers. It was my seventh and final year of elementary school. Next year I would be entering high school.

That fall and winter we played football and basketball, and when spring came we formed a baseball team and played games with other neighborhoods. The city playground teams were too high-powered for most of our players, so we decided to set up a league of our own. I mailed a notice about it to the newspaper sports page, and a half-dozen teams from all over Charleston asked to take part. Games were played at the far end of College Park. When our team was not playing, I umpired the games from behind the pitcher's mound, and afterward I telephoned in the scores, pitchers, and leading hitters for the next morning's paper. When the season was over, my parents gave a garden party for the winning teams—the only occasion in which they had shown any interest in the league. The afternoon newspaper sent a photographer, and the picture of the winners appeared on the sports page. So it turned out well.

MY FASCINATION WITH THE GAME of baseball has lasted for a lifetime. As for the particular events I have described, one might think that their emotional reverberations would long since have receded. yet they have not. The image of the left-handed glove priced at $1.25 on display at the hardware store endures in my memory. So too does the despair I felt as I watched the blue cardboard box disappear into the closet of my parents' bedroom. They have lasted, poignantly and keenly, over the years.

The reasons for their survival now seem obvious enough. My family's move had placed me in what had become an all-too-familiar situation. Once more I found myself in a new neighborhood, confronted with the need to make new friends, and with yet another change of schools lying ahead, just as had happened again and again since my father had first been taken to the hospital.

This time, however, my father had intervened to help me. Although preoccupied with his own adult problems of adjustment to a changed circumstance, he had been able to understand, as my mother had not, why for an eleven-year-old boy in Uptown Charleston, a proper baseball glove, one that would leave the throwing hand free, might seem important. Thus the exultation that I felt when the left-handed glove became mine was very likely compounded by the knowledge that my father had come to my rescue.

If so, then conversely my desolation when the glove was confiscated may have had a dimension that carried meaning beyond even the disappointment over its loss as such. What might also help to account for its impact was the demonstration that my father had allowed himself to be overruled by my mother. In any event the memory has been vivid for seventy-five years.

In thinking back over what happened—not only the incident of the left handed glove but the baseball league of the following summer as well—there is something else that occurs to me. This is that, not for the last time in my life, I had found a way to take part.

5

THE BOLL WEEVIL
AND THE TRIPLE PLAY

Summer afternoons when I sat in the bleachers along the third-base line and watched the Municipal League baseball games, I would look away sometimes and see the Boll Weevil standing at the station. I never saw it arrive. At some point during the early afternoon, I would glance over beyond the expanse of outfield, and it would be there. It was a small gas-electric combine, painted black with several smudged white stripes, containing operating cab, baggage room, and passenger compartment all in one, with a day coach coupled behind. Each day it came to Charleston, and after a lengthy wait at the little Seaboard Air Line station out beyond left field, it resumed its journey. And just as I never saw it arrive, but only looked up to see it there, so I never saw it leave. The ball game would reclaim my attention, and later when I would look again it would be gone.

"Boll Weevil" was not the little train's official title. The name arose because when the gas-electric combine, or "doodlebug" as the railroad men called it, was first placed in service, the black people of the region who constituted its principal patronage were reminded of the little bug that had virtually wiped out the Sea Island cotton industry some years earlier.

There were in fact not one but two daily Boll Weevils, one northbound for Hamlet, North Carolina, and the other southbound for Savannah, Georgia. The northbound train usually arrived about noontime and the southbound in midafternoon. The route through Charleston was not the Seaboard Railway's main line but a branch built to provide passenger and freight service for the little towns and crossroad points along the South Carolina coast. When once my father was to go to Savannah on business and I was to be taken along, I assumed that we would be going on the Boll Weevil, only to find that we drove instead up to North Charleston and boarded an Atlantic Coast Line train for the journey.

That was evidence, even for me at that age, of the humble position of the Boll Weevil. It was barely even a full-fledged train. Nobody I had ever known had ever ridden on it, anywhere. No stem locomotive, no Pullmans, no dining car—only the little gas-electric combine, a baggage car, and a lone day coach. It did not even use the Union Station Downtown, but only a small pink stucco station of its own.

College Park, where the Municipal League baseball games were played, and from where I could see the Boll Weevil at the station, was decidedly longer measured from north to south than east to west. The diamond and the bleachers were located in the southwest corner, so that to hit a home run over the right-field fence into the trees along Rutledge Avenue was only a relatively short poke. A ball hit to left field, however, might sail on and on and still come to earth within the limits of the playing field, for there was no left-field fence. Depending upon the velocity with which it traveled, it might roll all the way to the Seaboard parking lot for an inside-the-park home run.

Though Charleston in the mid-1930s was a city of some sixty-five thousand in population, there was no professional baseball team playing there nor had there been for some years. The old-timers used to speak in nostalgic memory of the Charleston Palmettos, who won the championship of the South Atlantic League back in 1922, a year before I was born, and whose lineup included no fewer than three soon-to-be major league stars: George Pipgras, who later pitched for the great New York Yankee Murderers Row teams of the late 1920s; Kiki Cuyler, outfielder for the Pittsburgh Pirates and Chicago Cubs and ultimately named to the Baseball Hall of Fame; and Lance Richbourg, who played on the Boston Braves for a number of years and later managed in the high minor leagues.

Those days, alas, were long gone. When the Great Depression came, the Sally League folded, and when it was revived, Charleston was not among the franchises. Watching baseball was a matter for me of watching the Sokol Tigers, Tru-Blu Brewers, Fort Moultrie Artillerymen, Garco Asbestosmen, and the other amateur teams in the Municipal League.

On hot days when the game was slow and one-sided, and the sun bore down from above, while the dense foliage of the trees in Hampton Park blocked off any breeze that might be blowing in off the Ashley River a mile away to the west, I would begin watching for the Boll Weevil. I knew that it would be coming across the bridge into the city, and would stop at the stucco station beyond left field. If it had been a freight train or had been pulled by a steam locomotive, I could have heard it coming, but the puttering of the gas-electric engine was unable to penetrate the noise of the baseball crowd.

I would resolve that this time I was actually going to catch sight of it as it pulled into the station, and not merely look at some point and see it standing there. But something always happened to divert my attention. The pace of the game picked up, or there was a commotion of some sort in the stands, or a dispute developed between the players and the umpires, and I would look away from the station, and when I remembered and turned back to watch once again, the Boll Weevil would have already arrived and would be there waiting.

Then I would vow that in any event I was going to see it make its departure. But it always remained at the station for so lengthy a wait that my patience failed me. I resumed watching the game, forgot about the little train, and only later looked back over toward the station to find it empty and deserted and the Boll Weevil gone off on its appointed journey.

IN THE BLEACHERS WERE a group of regulars, most of who could be counted upon to be present at almost every game. Together they observed the progress of the play and made sage remarks concerning its merits. There was old Mr. Lewis, who at about the turn of the century had played amateur and semipro ball along with the longtime Pittsburgh Pirate pitcher Babe Adams. There was Mr. Otto Kleinhagen, a huge man of some six feet three inches, and weighing at least 250 pounds, who was the night clerk at the police station. Mr. Kleinhagen was a jovial man, who liked to get on umpires. Soldier Edmondson and Harold Fortune, customarily the arbiters for all the Municipal League games, were made the target of repeated commentary. "Better sweep off home plate, Soldier!" Mr. Kleinhagen would call. "You can't see it, but the pitcher might like to know where it is!" Or if Harold Fortune had called a pitch to Mr. Kleinhagen's disapproval, "Harold, when you going to apply for one of them seeing-eye dogs?" Or, "you wouldn't know a strike if John L. Lewis was to call it!"

Since Mr. Kleinhagen, as a functionary of the police department, was involved in the enforcement of the law, it used to puzzle me just a little why he had so little sympathy for the umpires, who were also engaged in dispensing justice as best they could, without fear or favor. In baseball, however, Mr. Kleinhagen considered it no virtue for the law to be enforced blindly. He was inflexible and remorseless in his criticism.

Another regular performer in the bleachers was Alderman McKenna, a dignified-looking, ruddy-complexioned man, who always appeared at the games clad in straw hat and a seersucker suit with a bow tie and who never removed his coat no matter how fiercely the midsummer sun beamed down.

The alderman was a genial soul, and his chief activity during the game was to call out certain slogans, remarks, and comments at the appropriate moment. He had a supply of them, kept ready for each occasion. When the umpires first appeared on the playing field he would begin to chant "Three blind mice! Three blind mice!" If a batter swung mightily at a pitch but was able only to dribble a weak grounder toward the pitcher, he would call out, "Wipe the cranberry juice off it!" If a fan made a successful grab for a foul ball, the alderman's shouted response was always "Sign him up! Sign him up!"

One spectator who Alderman McKenna's repertory of responses never failed to delight was Mr. Sam Addleman, who ran a hardware store on upper King Street and who had a dry explosive laugh that resembled a quick burst from a machine gun. Whenever the alderman came forth with one of his remarks, Mr. Addleman could always be depended upon to respond with a salvo of staccato merriment, audible from one end of the bleachers to the other.

If an infielder made a high, leaping catch of a sharply-hit line drive, the alderman would shout "Look what *he* found!" and Mr. Addleman would fire off a volley of laughter. When a pitcher was being hit hard by the opposition, at the proper moment Alderman McKenna would sing out, "Take me out, Mister Manager, take me out!" and Mr. Addleman would respond appropriately. If a batter swung at a curve ball and missed emphatically, whirling his body around in the process, the alderman's call was always "put some oil on those rusty hinges!"—and the laugh would follow. If a player engaged in a heated dispute with the umpire over a call at the plate, when he finally came walking back sourly to the bench, Alderman McKenna would inevitably call out to him "Keep cool with Coolidge!"—with Mr. Addleman's brittle "Hah-hah-hah-hah-hah!" exploding instantly afterward.

The same assortment of spectators watched the same teams play week after week and even year after year, so everyone seemed to know all the players on all the teams. Each patron of the game had his favorites, those whose skills he most admired, and as these favorites performed there was debate over their relative merits.

My own favorite pitcher was not a fastballer, but a curve-balling control pitcher of rather slight build named Buzzard Burkholtz, who pitched for the Sokol Tigers. What was most striking about him was his delivery. He had a herky-jerky motion, and it came after a ferocious windup in which he flailed both his arms around like a windmill in a thunderstorm, so that when the pitch finally arrived at home plate it was almost in the nature of an afterthought.

Buzzard had a tendency to run out of energy in the late innings, however, and when he did and the hits began falling, the response of the crowd was predictable. "Hey, Buzzard, your cousins up there are waiting for your arm!" someone would call, pointing to imaginary buzzards in the sky. He was certainly not the best or the most talented of the pitchers in the Municipal League, but none worked harder than he did or expended so much motion and energy in delivering the ball to the plate.

In an odd way he reminded me of the little Boll Weevil train. Perhaps it was only my imagination, or perhaps it was because he gave up so many long fly balls to left field that when he was pitching, I would find myself looking out more often in that direction. It seemed to me that when he was the pitcher the little black combine was always likely to be standing there at the Seaboard station.

BOTH THE YOUNG AND THE moderately old played baseball in the Municipal League. It was by no means unusual for several of the better players on the high-school team to win positions in the lineups, while at the same time there were several whose baseball experience went back fifteen years and more, into the dead-ball era before the coming of Babe Ruth.

There was one young player who was not only an exceptionally graceful fielder and an effective pitcher, but he hit the ball often and for distance. There was general agreement that he was destined for a career in professional baseball. The story was that several major league clubs had their eyes on him and that he had already been approached with contract offers, but that he planned to go to college instead.

One day the sports page of the Sunday newspaper, the *News and Courier,* bore a headline, set in eight columns across the page: "YANKEE SCOUT HERE TO WATCH EDDIE SHOKES." The story announced that a bona fide scout for the New York Yankees was in Charleston for the express purpose of seeing young Eddie Shokes play for the Tru-Blu Brewers that afternoon.

The idea of a major league scout, and representing the New York Yankees at that, actually being here in Charleston to view a local player was astounding to me. I had never seen even a minor league professional baseball game played, let alone a major league team like the Yankees. It was as if a thing remote and fabulous, of a dimension of importance far too vast to have anything to do with a small southern city such as mine, had abruptly appeared before me—as if I were to look up casually during a Municipal League game and see standing at the Seaboard station beyond left field not the familiar little Boll Weevil but a magnificent compound-articulated steam locomotive, with double sets of drive wheels, enormous pistons and great drive rods, and the name "UNION PACIFIC RAILROAD" lettered across its tender.

When game time came, there was a sell-out crowd in the bleachers, and the nonpaying spectators lined the wire outfield fences four and five deep. Naturally I hoped that I could actually catch sight of the Yankee scout at the game, but wherever it was that he was seated, he did not look different enough from other persons in attendance for me to detect who he was.

There was an interview in the *News and Courier* the next morning in which the Yankee scout was quoted as saying that young Eddie Shokes was indeed a fine prospect and that he would be back again later in the season to observe him further.

As it turned out, Shokes signed a contract with the Cincinnati Reds and played briefly in the National League before and after the Second World War, but he never proved able to hit big league pitching consistently. Alone of all those players in the Municipal League, however, he had made it to the majors.

IT WAS SHORTLY AFTER THE YANKEE scout had come to look at Eddie Shokes that I saw my first professional baseball game. Up in Richmond, Virginia, where my mother grew up and where I had grandparents, aunts, uncles, and cousins, there were the Richmond Colts of the Class-B Pied-mont League. When an invitation arrived for me to spend a week in that city, I was most excited at the prospect, and not least because I would be traveling there and back on the train—not the little Boll Weevil of the Seaboard Air Line, but one of the crack Florida-to-New York trains of the Atlantic Coast Line, which I had seen occasionally when they put in at the North Charleston station ten miles north of town.

Sometimes on Sunday afternoons in the fall and winter my parents would take my younger brother and sister and myself out to North Charleston to watch the northbound and southbound Havana Specials come in and depart. But this time, when the northbound train departed, I would be on board. It mattered that the train was northbound, headed up the Atlantic coast toward the big cities, Washington, Baltimore, Philadel-phia, most of all New York City itself. It was true that I was only going as far as Richmond, but the train itself would be traveling all the way so that as long as I was aboard it I could think of myself as riding on a New York–bound train.

If the actuality of the train trip to Richmond were not enough, I pre-tended that it was a half-dozen years later and I had become a star ballplayer. Now the major leagues were beckoning, and of course I would go like this, on the Atlantic Coast Line train, up to the North and New York City and the Polo Grounds, to become a .300-hitting first baseman for the New York Giants, putting far behind me College Park, the Municipal League, and the little Boll Weevil waiting at the Seaboard station.

It was on the third night of my visit in Richmond that I went to the baseball game. An uncle took me; we rode the streetcar all the way from Robinson Street down Main Street to Fourteenth, then walked down along the bridge to Mayo's Island in the James River, where the ballpark was sit-uated. It was the first night game I had ever seen, and it was played in a true baseball park, with tiers of floodlights to illuminate the playing field far more brightly than the lights under which softball games were played in Charleston. There were wooden outfield fences with signs painted on them, ticket windows, turnstiles, a covered grandstand as well as bleacher seats, a scoreboard, a public-address system playing music as the crowd filed in, passageways and concession stands, printed scorecards, dugouts for the home and visiting teams instead of wooden benches along the fence as at College Park, and in right centerfield atop the scoreboard a flagpole with an American flag and a pennant emblematic of the fact that the Richmond Colts had won the Piedmont League championship.

Everything about the game was impressive. The team uniforms resembled those of the major league players that I saw pictured in newspapers and magazines. What I found most impressive of all was the knowledge that these were professional baseball players; it was entirely possible that within several years some of them might indeed be playing regularly in the major leagues.

The play of the infielders seemed better than that in the Municipal League. The second baseman and shortstops made stops of hard grounders that I felt sure would have gone through for hits back home. Back home such a display of skill would have brought the crowd to its feet, and the cheering would have lasted a full minute or longer. Here, however, though the crowd applauded, the way the double play was executed did not seem to be considered so very remarkable. In fact a man seated in back of us remarked that the second baseman should have been playing deeper.

In the second inning, one of the Durham batters hit a looping foul fly over into the bleachers just beyond first base, and when one of the spectators reached out and caught it, there was an instant cry of "Sign him up!" A little later the Richmond shortstop leaped high in the air to spear a sharply hit line drive over his shoulder, and a man seated below us in the stands called out, "Look what *he* found!" Could it also be, I thought, that if either of the pitchers got into trouble, somebody might begin singing, "Take me out, Mister Manager, take me out"?

The discovery that Alderman McKenna's witty sayings were not original to him and to the Municipal League came along with another and somewhat different discovery. Because the lights illuminating the playing field were so bright, it was difficult for me to make out anything at all in the darkness beyond the outfield walls. Several times I heard train whistles and what must have been long strings of freight trains rumbling by, over toward the Richmond side of Mayo's Island, but could see no sign of them.

Then at one point during the game I happened to look out beyond right field, and saw what appeared to be the beam of a light shining atop what was evidently a railroad trestle. The cone of the light grew narrower and more focused, until after a minute I could see the outline of a locomotive itself in the darkness, its headlamp illuminating the track ahead, with the light from the firebox throwing an orange glare into the cloud of smoke just above it.

As I watched, there came into view a long string of yellow squares, resembling the lighted windows of the trolley-car parades we used to stage when I was a small child, in which we would cut small squares in the cardboard sides of shoe boxes, attach strings to them, place lighted candle stumps inside, and pull them along the sidewalk. What I was looking at were the lighted windows of a long passenger train moving across a viaduct.

"What railroad is that?" I asked, and was told that it was a train on the Seaboard Air Line, bound for the Main Street Station downtown in Richmond. So the Seaboard as well as the Atlantic Coast Line had full-fledged passenger trains with strings of day coaches and Pullmans and diners, even if they did not pass through Charleston. Its passenger trains were not restricted to little gas-electric combines like the Boll Weevil.

THE WEEKEND FOLLOWING my return home I went to see the Sunday doubleheader at College Park. In the first game the Sokol Tigers were playing the Tru-Blu Brewers.

Buzzard Burkhardt was pitching for Sokol. His windmill windup, which I had always admired, now seemed herky-jerky and amateurish by comparison with the pitchers I had seen in Richmond. The players in general seemed to lack professional authority. There was a feeling of casualness to all, as if it were only a game—which of course was just what it was. In part this may have been because I was watching from close to the playing field, not from high up in the grandstand as in Richmond. There was more to it than that, however. What the Municipal League game lacked was Importance. Careers and future expectations did not seem at stake.

Yet as the game wore on, I grew accustomed to it again, and ceased to think in terms of how the players, the play, and the ballpark itself compared with what I had seen up in Richmond a few nights earlier.

In the ninth inning, a hit dropped in front of the Sokol Tigers centerfielder, and then Buzzard gave up a base on balls, placing the tying run on second. The next batter lined a terrific shot over second base.

Instantly, as I watched, the Sokol shortstop made a diving leap, speared the ball for the out, flipped it to the second baseman to double the runner off second, and the second baseman fired it over to first base. *A triple play!*

For a long moment there was absolute silence. Then everyone began to yell. They stood on their feet and shouted their praise. As the Sokol Tigers came off the field and the bench, they were hugging each other, pounding the shortstop and second baseman on the back, waving and shouting in triumph. Few of those present, spectators and players alike, had ever actually seen a triple play before. Even in the major leagues they were rare enough; in the Municipal League it was an unprecedented event.

Later on, just before the second game started, I happened to look out toward left field, and saw the Boll Weevil. It was standing at the station, with its single day coach coupled behind the cab-engine-baggage combine. I felt, rather agreeably, that I was back in my own country again.

6

FINISTERRE

> Although more and more people are coming to refer to boats with
> the neuter pronoun "it," the traditional "she" remains fully correct
> in speaking or writing about any size of vessel.
>
> Chapman, *Piloting, Seamanship, and Small Boat Handling*, 58th ed.

The marshland along the Ashley River shoreline was several hundred yards
across. It stretched northward and southward until out of sight. At low tide
it was a thick carpet of reed grass and stalks, green from late spring well
into the fall, turning sallow and dun in winter and remaining so through
April and much of May. At flood tide the river water covered all but the tips
of the grass, transforming the surface of the marsh into a mirrorlike image
of the sky overhead.

Several times a week freighters and tugboats came by along the ship
channel, bound for the industrial installations that lay upstream and out of
sight from our front porch or returning downstream to the ocean. By far
the greater part of the city's maritime activity, however, took place along
the Cooper River waterfront Downtown, close to where the two rivers
joined to form the harbor.

Our house was located on a bluff at the foot of Sans Souci Street, not
far from the northern city limits. Once we were moved in, I began exploring our new surroundings. I made my way along the shoreline, followed
trails through the thickets and brambles, climbed up onto the limbs of
water oaks reaching out over the banks, and observed the waterfowl out in
the marshland.

There were creeks through the reed grass, flowing and ebbing as the
tide rose and fell. When tide was out, only a trickle of water was left in the

creek beds, but the thick black mud along the exposed roots of the reed grass along banks on either side afforded no footing whatever. As the tide came in, the water filled the creeks and spread over into the reed grass, and in periods of more than ordinary high water covered it over. There was a small dock at the head of a creek at the foot of the bluff, from which we could net crabs.

In the spring the reeds turned green from the roots up. First a band of pale green appeared in the otherwise drab matting, then crept upwards as the weeks passed, giving the neutral tones of the marsh a green shading that became wider and deeper, until from shoreline to river's edge there was almost solid greenness.

What I wanted to do was to paddle a rowboat out to the river-most edge of the marsh, so that when a ship came along I could observe from close by. Not only was no rowboat available, however, but there was also the inconvenient fact that I did not know how to swim. Lessons at the YMCA had been to no avail. Not even individual sessions with the swimming instructor, a man with the odd name of Fudge, could persuade me to turn loose the railing of the pool. I had tried again and again, to no avail.

So I was landbound—which, however, served only to increase my interest in the occasional ships passing by out in the river channel and the tugboats that accompanied them. I watched through my father's binoculars as they moved along, and I identified the individual tugs by name. I looked for the home ports of the ships, lettered across the stern, and speculated on their far-off destinations. In fact most of them bore cargoes of phosphate rock and Chilean nitrate or carried away creosoted lumber from a wood-preserving plant.

MEANWHILE THE NEIGHBORHOOD, now that it had been opened up for development, was gaining new residents. Streets and roads were being cut through the fields, and homes were under construction, including several close to our own. Sans Souci Street was unpaved, but street lamps were installed at intersections. There was talk of sidewalks being poured and of house-to-house mail delivery replacing the cluster of mail boxes presently mounted on a corner four blocks to the east.

The High School of Charleston was located Downtown, and getting there involved a six-block hike to the Rutledge Avenue streetcar line and a three-mile ride to school. There were no junior high schools; seven years of elementary school were followed by four of high school. So by the time I turned fourteen, I was well into my sophomore year.

Sometimes on Saturdays, after attending Sabbath school Downtown, I walked down to the Cooper River waterfront on my own. The *Cherokee,* one of the coastal passenger ships, would usually be tied up at the Clyde Line wharves, in full view from the shore. From there I walked southward, past a marine-repair yard and the mud-imbedded remains of several abandoned hulks, to Adger's Wharf.

In actuality it was two wharves and served as home for a variety of shrimp trawlers, workboats, and a few pleasure craft. By far its most interesting residents were the tugboats of the White Stack Towboat Company. There were three of them, brick red with white trimming and glossy black hulls and with tall white smokestacks topped in black. They were maintained in prime condition and, when not at work about the harbor, lay alongside the south wharf, boilers always kept fired, with wisps of smoke trailing from their stacks.

It was a bracing sight to view the tugs departing or returning, their powerful propellers churning the harbor water into foamy little hills as they maneuvered alongside the pier. If assigned to dock an incoming ship, one of them set out down the waterfront and past the Battery, then steered eastward along the James Island shore to meet it out by the quarantine station, while another waited out in the channel for its arrival off the Battery to accompany it to the piers upstream.

Ships calling at Charleston normally tied up at the Union Terminal wharves along the Cooper River. These were screened from view from the shore behind warehouses of corrugated metal with high chain-link fences around them. Further up the shore was the United Fruit Company wharf, where there was often a ship with white hull and superstructure, part of the Great White Fleet, unloading bananas from Central America. The Great White Fleet carried passengers as well as bananas, though I believe not out of Charleston. I had seen the advertisements in the *National Geographic.* To travel aboard one of its ships southward down the Atlantic coast, around the tip of Florida, and across the Gulf of Mexico down to a port in the tropics, and to watch as it took on a fresh cargo, would surpass my most extravagant hopes.

In early June the high school year ended. I was fourteen and in the fall would be a junior. Now there was time for everything. Baseball season was in full tilt. Among families moving into our neighborhood there were several persons my own age, including a girl my sister knew named Janet Bonnoit. She was small, with black hair and gray-green eyes. Sometimes in the evenings my sister and I went over to Janet Bonnoit's house, and several times we rode our bicycles over to the clay courts on Hampton Park Terrace and played tennis.

ONE DAY IN EARLY JULY I bicycled all the way down to the Cooper River waterfront. Two of the White Stack tugboats were missing from Adger's Wharf, an indication that they were upstream docking or undocking a ship. I rode over to the High Battery to wait for developments. A breeze was blowing in from the southeast, and the surface of the harbor was choppy. After a time a freighter came into view from behind the wharves, out in the channel off Castle Pinckney, with the tugboats following. They cruised past the Battery. Afterward the bow waves came crashing into the rocks at the base of the seawall.

Once the ship turned eastward toward Fort Sumter and the harbor entrance, the tugs swung away, their assignment completed. The ship continued on, its hull pointed seaward, smoke fanning out from its tall funnel, its broad rounded stern in full sight. I had the sense that the ship, its business with the shore done, was returning to its proper element. If when moving past the Battery with the tugs it had looked clumsy and cumbrous, it now took on a capability of its own. It moved beyond Fort Johnson at the end of James Island, passed between Fort Sumter and the Sullivan's Island shoreline, and eventually, by the time it headed for the entrance at the harbor jetties and the ocean beyond, it was no more than a receding silhouette. Watching it dwindle into the distance I felt a sense of an opportunity missed, as if a cloud had drifted over the sun.

ON A DAY NOT LONG afterward, I sat out on our front porch talking with a schoolmate who lived six blocks away. The tide was more than usually high that afternoon, covering much of the marsh grass, so that there appeared to be almost an unbroken sheet of water between the shoreline and the Ashley River itself. I remarked how much I wished I had a boat so that we could paddle out to the edge of the river. My friend, whose name was John Connolly, agreed. Maybe we could build a boat, he suggested.

The more I thought about it—and I thought about it from then on—the better the idea seemed. After dark that evening, we paid a visit to a house under construction not far from mine. Working underneath our side porch, within a couple of days we had nailed together a flat-bottomed skiff, blunt at both ends, unpainted, eight feet long and thirty inches across, with high sides, and planks for seats.

My sister and Janet Bonnoit came by to inspect. "That's a boat?" my sister asked.

"Yes."

"Which end is the front?"

"It can go either way. Whichever way we paddle it."

"And you're going out in the river in *that?*"

"Not the river," I said, "the marsh. It's meant for paddling around in."

"Oh, I'd like to go," Janet Bonnoit declared.

"Not me," my sister said.

My father also briefly observed what we were doing. "If you go out in that, you'd better take along some bailing cans," he said.

At suppertime I was careful to avoid making any reference to the boat. If my mother knew what was going on, she said nothing.

By early afternoon the day following, the boat was ready for launching. It was heavy. We managed to lift it onto my brother's wagon and to maneuver it out of our yard and down the bluff to the dock.

We eased the boat off the wagon and onto the wharf, tied a clothesline rope to it, and pushed it into the creek. The boat slid out into the current.

"It floats," John announced. Until then neither of us had been quite sure that it would.

I pulled the boat back against the dock, handed the rope to John, and climbed in. The boat swayed a little, but seemed safe beneath my step. I sat down on one of the seat planks, John followed, and we took up the paddles we had nailed together.

"Hey, it's leaking!" John said. Creek water was jetting in along the seams in little fountains.

"I'll bail and you paddle," I said. I began dipping out water with the coffee can, while John pushed with his paddle to turn the boat around until one end was pointing down the creek.

"Anchors aweigh!" he declared. We set out along the creek. After a minute I looked back at the dock. It was now some distance away.

We continued along the creek until we arrived at a place where we could turn out into the wider area of flooded marsh. The tips of the reed grass brushed against the hull as we eased into it. We bailed out more water, then let the boat drift while we looked around.

I could see our house back up the bluff through the oak trees. Someone was standing on the porch watching. Upriver some wharves, until now blocked from view by the oak trees along the shore, were visible and what appeared to be the masts of a ship. Downriver we could see all the way to the Seaboard railway trestle.

The water kept coming in, and we took turns bailing and paddling. "We're going to have to do something about these leaks," John said.

"Let's go back to the dock," I said.

We paddled across the flooded marsh and back along the creek. with intervals of bailing en route. At the dock we climbed out, tied the clothes-line to the dock, and stood watching the boat rocking in the tide. There it was—shaped like a shoebox, given much too much to leaking, but a boat. With it I had ventured out into the marshland at last.

Now that I had been seen out in the boat, it could be mentioned openly, and at supper I described its performance in glowing terms. My mother appeared to have accepted the inevitable. "You'd better be careful," she said. "If you fell in you wouldn't be able to swim." I assured her that there was no danger of my falling in, and that even if I did I would be safe enough in the marsh.

During the night there was another high tide. When I went down to the dock after breakfast the tide was out and the boat was resting along the edge of the marsh grass across the creek, largely out of the water, the clothesline still tied to the dock. There were several inches of water inside.

John Connolly came over early in the afternoon. The tide had flowed back in, and the boat was once again afloat in the creek, with water still in the hull. We bailed it out, climbed aboard, and again set out down the creek. Water was still seeping in, but notably less slowly than the day before; the planks were evidently swelling. We paddled the boat out into the marsh again. However wetly, our project was a success. Now if only a ship would come by. But none did.

After a few days, John Connolly lost interest in paddling around in the marsh. I went exploring on my own, following rivulets leading off the creek, some so narrow that I had to pole my way along. There were some days when even at high tide the water in the creek rose so little that when standing up in the boat I could scarcely see over the top of the reed grass, and I seemed almost to be paddling along tunnels. If there was no wind, the marsh could be very hot and sticky, with the reed grass screening off any breeze. Occasionally I would come upon hordes of little white insects, which swarmed hotly around me, and I would have to use the paddle as a pole to get the boat out of range as swiftly as possible.

At other times, as I threaded my way along, there would be a sudden splash and flurry of wings up ahead, and a heron or a marsh hen, alarmed at my unexpected appearance, would lift into the air and go winging off across the marsh.

The days I liked best were those with very high tides, for then I did not have to confine my explorations to the creeks. At such times there seemed almost nowhere in the salt marsh that I could not go. The edge of the Ashley River itself was about a quarter mile from the shore. I did not venture there, however. It would be a long way to paddle, for the creek did not flow in a straight line but had bends and curves. Nor did I know how powerful the current along the river might be, or whether I would be able to keep the squared bow pointed into the current. There might be waves and eddies that could spin the boat around. What it came down to was that I was afraid of the water.

ON AN AFTERNOON IN LATE July, I resolved to paddle far enough down the creek to where I could at least see the mouth and the river flowing past. There was one bend in the creek at which its boundaries became noticeably wider, and at that I always turned back. This time I kept going.

Soon the creek was twenty-five feet or more across from bank to bank, and the flow was moving through the reed stalks downstream, pushing briskly against the boat. The current was bearing me along. Up ahead another bend was in sight. The mouth of the creek and the open river might well lie just beyond it.

Yet, almost before I knew it, I had turned back, and was paddling shoreward. I did not ease up on until the river current flowing through the reed grass had slackened off and was no longer shoving at the side of the boat.

Then I lay down the paddle, picked up the bailing can, and began scooping out water, even though there was really no need to do so yet. I was breathing heavily.

Involuntarily, automatically, the moment I felt that I was losing control of the boat's motion, I had given in to panic. It had been like the swimming lessons at the YMCA or my precipitate bolt from the reception at the Jewish Community Center.

From downriver, out of sight beyond the Seaboard railroad trestle, there was the wail of a tugboat klaxon, followed by the low growl of a ship's whistle, blowing for the trestle to open. I thought of pulling over into the reed grass and waiting to see whether the trestle span would swing open and a tug and freighter emerge. It would be a lengthy wait, however, and by the time ship and tug drew close the tide would have turned and the water begun draining out of the creek and the marsh. So I paddled on back toward the dock. From downriver, below the Seaboard trestle, almost as if in derision, the ship's whistle hooted again.

My sister's friend Janet Bonnoit remarked again one evening that she would like to go out in the boat. We were at her house listening to the *Lucky Strike Hit Parade* on the radio, and I was talking about how I hoped to see a ship pass by on the river while I was out in the marsh on the boat.

"Not in that boat," my sister said. "It leaks."

"It's not bad any more. The planks have swelled up."

"Then why do you have to take your shoes off and leave them on the dock?"

"I don't have to. I just like to go barefoot."

"So do I," Janet Bonnoit said. "I've always wanted to go to the edge of the river!"

She really does want to, I thought. "It still leaks a little," I admitted. "But not like at first."

"Oh, I'd like to go," she repeated. "Couldn't I come along sometime? I could bail while you paddle. Satisfaction guaranteed!"

The upshot was that we would go out in the boat the next afternoon if the weather was good.

"Hah!" my sister declared on the way home.

"You can come too if you want," I offered. "You can take turns."

"Not in that boat I won't."

"You would if it was John Connolly instead of me."

"Hah!"

The prospect was exciting. It was what I had hoped might happen, I knew, when I introduced the topic. It would be like going on a date. I had never been out on a date.

My sister began humming "Red Sails In The Sunset": "Oh, carry my loved one back safely to me."

I WAS A LONG TIME IN getting to asleep. I heard the Seaboard Air Line freight train materialize from far out in St. Andrews Parish, rumble across the trestle, and ultimately disappear into the city. The Rutledge Avenue streetcars droned their way uptown and to the end of the line at Magnolia Crossing, then back downtown again. I plotted my actions for the next day. I told myself again and again that I must not halt until the open river itself was fully in sight.

When eventually I did fall asleep I dreamed that I was walking along a path, which I recognized as one that led from the streetcar station on Hampton Park Terrace, where we had lived years before. Nor far away was a thick grove of bamboo with some oleander bushes. I could hear footsteps along the gravel path behind me. It was a girl, carrying a package under her arm. I recognized her. In the seventh grade at James Simons School, her desk had been across from mine. I could not remember her name, but someone had said that she went out for walks with boys at night.

"Are you going to the parade?" she asked. I knew she was referring to the dress parade at the Citadel, at the west of Hampton Park. "If you are we'd better hurry. I know a shortcut. Come with me!"

A narrow pathway led into an opening in the bamboo grove. Inside a clothesline rope was strung along one side. "Hold onto the rope," she said; "it gets real dark in here." I followed along behind her. Soon only a glimmer of daylight was coming through the bamboo.

"Are you sure this is a shortcut?" I asked.

"Satisfaction guaranteed!" she said.

I thought I could hear drums throbbing. Some distance away there was a noise like a cannon being fired. The sunset gun, I thought. We would be too late for the parade.

In the dark the girl stumbled, and the rope we were holding onto gave way. She fell against me, sending us both sprawling. As we struggled to get to our feet there was a beam of yellow light, and I could make out the words on the lid of the package she had been carrying, which now lay on the ground: ONSLOW'S DIVINITY FUDGE. Onslow's was a candy store downtown on King Street.

There was another cannon boom, this time so close by that it shook the ground.

I blinked my eyes from the light and sat up. I was in my room, and my father was closing the windows next to my bed. Outside the rain was coming down, and there was another flash, then a crack of thunder. "We've missed the parade," I said.

My father trained the flashlight on me. "There's no parade," he said. "It was raining in. Go back to sleep." He turned the light away.

The rain was ratting away up on the roof above my head. I thought about it for a moment, then I closed my eyes in the darkness.

WHEN JANET BONNOIT came down the bluff to the dock the next afternoon, I had the boat bailed out and ready to go. It had taken on some rain water, but the line had held firmly. The tide was well up into the reed grass, and there were ripples on the surface of the creek. The day was bright with a high sky and scattered white clouds. We set out along the creek.

By the time we reached the bend where I had turned back, the boat was swaying in the current, and there was a little water in the hull. I felt the cross-flow from the marsh shoving against the side, moving us toward the bank. This time I gripped the paddle tightly and kept paddling.

The creek was now quite wide. We were moving steadily along. We turned into another bend, entered it, and in view up ahead of us was the river itself.

I paddled for the side of the creek, and we glided up into the reed grass. The cross-flow was pushing the boat further into the marsh. I lowered the rope with the window sashes into the water. After a few seconds the forward movement through the reed grass ceased, and we were holding in place.

If not at the rim of the river, we could see it clearly. Nearer to the edge of the river the creek divided into two channels, with a delta between them partly covered over with grass. I could see the spears of reed grass along the fringes, dipping and bending in the flow. Beyond, the river flowed by.

"It's so beautiful out here," Janet declared. "Wouldn't it be great if we could go all the way across to the other side!" The salt marsh along the western shore lay a quarter mile away, and beyond that a dark green belt of trees.

"Not in a little boat like this," I said at once. I was less interested in the scenery than in our stability. The downstream flow was coursing through the reed stalks, and the boat rocked back and forth. There was a half inch of water in the boat. I set to work scooping it out with the coffee can.

"Look!" Janet said after a minute, pointing upstream.

A mile away, off the industrial docks a ship was out in the river, its bow pointed in our direction. A tugboat was alongside it.

I thought of the ships and tugs I had watched passing by the High Battery and how the waves from the wake had come crashing against the rocks along the seawall below. "We'd better go further back in the marsh," I said, and began hauling on the anchor rope.

Once the window sashes were back inside the hull, I lost no time in pushing back out into the creek and turning shoreward. It was slow going, but after a minute we began to make headway. Once we rounded the bend we moved along more decisively.

A few minutes later, and I was nosing the boat back into the reed grass, this time with a belt of marshland between us and the edge of the river. The creek delta was no longer in view. From our new vantage point I could see the tugboat and the ship moving down the river channel.

Not far from us in the marsh was a piling the thickness of a telephone pole and seven or eight feet long. It must have come loose from a wharf somewhere upstream, I thought. There were barnacles along one end. Perhaps the next extra-high tide would carry it back out into the river and let it continue on its way to the sea. Meanwhile the creek current swirled around it.

The ship and escort were drawing nearer. We waited in the marsh. I could recognize the tug as the *Robert H. Lockwood,* which I had often seen at Adger's Wharf. As it passed opposite us there was a crewman standing at the stern. Janet waved her hand. He waved back.

The freighter drew abreast, running empty, high-sided and stately, waterline in view. The hull was painted bright green, with the cabin, cargo booms, and masts yellow, and the funnel black with a thin green stripe. Everything—wheelhouse, a lifeboat attached to davits, companionway ladders, air vents, deck machinery, the portholes along the hull—was clearly visible, out in the ship channel less than a hundred yards away. Below the broad rounded stern, the propeller thumped slowly, half out of the water. Above the stern deck was a tricolor flag. As the freighter moved downstream I read the lettering:

FINISTERRE

BORDEAUX

The wake was spreading out from the bow, and the wave crests rolled into the marsh one after another, surging into the reed grass and spreading along the creek in little ridges. Our boat swayed as it lifted and dropped.

The oncoming processional diminished, and the surface of the creek became calmer. Up ahead of us the piling, sprung loose from the reed stalks by the flooding water, had swung out, until the barnacled end was part way into the creek.

Out of sight along the edge there was a lessening sequence of splashes as the wake arrived at the marsh downstream in successive waves, each farther away. We watched the stern of the outbound *Finisterre* recede down the channel, bound for the harbor and the high seas, the *Robert H. Lockwood* leading the way.

WHEN THE HIGH SCHOOL term began in mid-September, my excursions with the boat grew infrequent. Once I did actually go out into the river itself, taking along an inflated inner tube for a life preserver. My intention was to paddle upstream along the edge of the marsh, then let the current float the boat back downstream to the mouth of the creek. The boat proved to be very difficult to keep pointed into the river current, however, and after some minutes of strenuous paddling I gave up the attempt. If I ever acquired a skiff that could be rowed instead of paddled, I would try it again.

In early October there was a storm, lasting a day and a night, with heavy rains and strong winds that knocked limbs down from the oak trees along the bluff. Afterward, when I went down to see how the boat had fared, it was gone. A severed length of frayed clothesline trailed in the creek.

LATE THAT FALL A LARGE green Corps of Engineers harbor dredge stationed itself out in the river, together with a flotilla of launches and barges. Soon an array of bright-colored pennants were in view in the marshland, and not long after that a network of connected pipes, mounted on floats, was discharging sediment into the marsh. The result—after more than a month of clanking, grinding, ringing of bells, and tooting of whistles and horns—was a line of white sand islands upstream and downstream along the marsh, effectively shutting off the creeks from the river.

Perhaps when summer came again I could build another boat, make my way across the marsh to the sand islands, and walk along the edge of the channel itself. I could even invite Janet Bonnoit to come along. I had finally taken her to the movies. For the present, however, the spring baseball season lay just ahead, and I had other things to think about.

7

"Do You Know Your Charleston?"

I was a senior in high school when, for the first time in my life, I was exposed to authors in full battle array at a literary reception. The exposure took place in the library of the High School of Charleston, and because of that it would prove to be atypical for such events, in that the refreshments served that afternoon were nonalcoholic. Otherwise the ingredients were standard.

It was not that I was unacquainted with writers. One of my uncles was a playwright who had several plays produced on Broadway. Another was the city editor of the afternoon newspaper. They and my father had grown up with a family friend whose stories appeared regularly in magazines and books.

The authors in attendance at the high school library that day, however, were of a different kind, or, more accurately, were present in a different role. They were there as Charleston Authors. It was not only that they written and published books, but that the city of Charleston was a recognizable presence in those books.

Thereby hangs a tale, the convolutions of which I would come to understand only later.

DURING THE SCHOOL YEAR before the reception, the High School of Charleston had celebrated its one hundredth anniversary. The observance had been scheduled to close with a gala historical pageant, oratory, music, presentation of awards and honors, and conferral of diplomas upon the graduating seniors. Unfortunately the advent of a polio epidemic in late spring necessitated a city-wide ban on public gatherings involving the young, so the program had to be cancelled.

When in September of 1939 a new school year began, the announcement was made that another celebratory event was in prospect. Its theme was to be "Do You Know Your Charleston?" In preparation for it, books about Charleston would be read and discussed in English classes, trips would be taken by history classes to visit appropriate historical and cultural sites, and student exhibits would be prepared and displayed. The project would culminate with a reception in honor of Charleston's authors. A committee of senior students would function as hosts. As editor of the student newspaper I was among those appointed to it.

A celebration of the city's past was not of itself a remarkable activity. The slogan of the Chamber of Commerce, the nation's oldest, was "America's Most Historic City," and the historical and architectural heritage of Charleston was its prime component. The title of a novel by a local author, *Look Back to Glory*, could be said to exemplify the importance of the tourist trade to the Downtown economy.

Newspaper and magazine articles made much of the continuing presence of the past. Each Sunday's *News and Courier* displayed a feature entitled "Do You Know Your Charleston?" In the spring, when the gardens were in bloom, the Downtown streets were crowded with tourists. Antique shops, art studios, flower vendors, and souvenir stands, sightseeing tours, harbor cruises, and outdoor markets flourished.

(A sizeable segment of the local population, those who were black, would have emphatically disagreed with the notion that the city's colonial and pre–Civil War existence had constituted any kind of historical Golden Age, but this would never have occurred to me or my schoolmates.)

I was told years afterward by a teacher who had been faculty adviser of the school newspaper that the immediate impetus was a visit to the school scheduled for later that autumn by an accreditation committee of the South Carolina State Board of Education. It seems that there was some apprehension among the faculty and administration that the curriculum being offered to the students might be, however mistakenly, thought to be insufficiently adventurous by some of those who would be doing the certifying.

The inspection committee, it was assumed, would very likely be made up of specialists holding graduate degrees in secondary education. Given that particular specialty, almost by definition a majority would doubtless be either high school administrators in upstate South Carolina or else professors of education at the state university. The thing to do would be to arrange for a student project to take place during their visit that would impress such persons.

The obvious choice of subject, proposed by one faculty member who was himself a former semipro baseball pitcher from upstate, would be the historical and cultural glories of Charleston. A classroom focus upon these was sure to result in an abundance of student work to go on display. A reception could be staged for the city's authors, and their books placed on exhibit.

An additional consideration was that the early flourishing of arts, architecture, and letters in and about Charleston dated back well before much of the upcountry had emerged from the stump-clearing, subsistence farming era. This, along with an appearance by the contemporary Charleston authors, would not only make an impression on the visiting educators, but perhaps even intimidate them a little—though nobody put it quite that way.

SO THE "DO YOU KNOW Your Charleston?" project was announced and got under way. The results began to appear in reading lists and on classroom walls and bulletin boards. Thereafter it gathered momentum. A list of local authors to be invited to the reception was drawn up. Whenever possible the invitations were delivered in person by groups of students. Seniors would be expected to attend the reception and mingle with the authors.

By the time that the State Board of Education's certification committee arrived in early December, there were exhibits everywhere; books and publications by and about Charleston authors were on display, and classroom blackboards, hallways, and office doors were lined with book jackets, posters, and photographs.

ORDINARILY I DISLIKED being made to take part in social functions. I felt awkward and graceless at them and, when spoken to, never knew what to say in reply. This time, however, it would be different. The guests would be Charleston Authors. I was on the committee to receive them. They would be talking about their writing, telling about authors they knew personally, and answering questions. Someone might even inquire about my own interest in writing, and tell me about books I should read.

On the appointed afternoon I was on hand at the high school library, attired in coat and tie for the occasion. When the guests began arriving, each author was greeted by the teachers and ushered to a strategic spot where that person's writings were on display. Soon groups of students and teachers were clustered about them. Tea was poured by faculty wives. Some took sugar and cream; some preferred lemon.

Several of the writers possessed what I thought was a definite "author-ial" appearance; others were more conventional in dress and look. There was one author with a bristling beard, dark, deep-set eyes that seemed almost to gleam, and a resounding voice, who gestured expansively as he spoke. Another, tall and red-haired with a ruddy complexion, had an out-doorsy appearance about him. I listened in on his conversation; he was talking about alligators.

A jovial, round-faced man in a tweed coat, with a shock of snow-white hair and a red bowtie, was describing the recent premiere of the movie of *Gone with the Wind* in Atlanta, which he had attended. Obviously he knew its author personally, for he referred to her as "Peggy." When the librarian came by he kissed her on both cheeks. One of the women authors present had on a formidable, broad-brimmed bonnet with flowers on it, which as she talked away oscillated vigorously overhead. Another, a tiny woman with silvery hair in ringlets, wore a velvet gown, ear pendants, a lengthy string of pearls, and silver bracelets on both arms.

I stood by for awhile, watching the proceedings and listening to the buzz of conversation. Any expectation that I might be able to discuss writ-ing with any of the authors appeared to be quite out of the question. I would have had to break into the flow of what was being said, and others more fluent and bolder than I were already occupying the attention of the visiting writers. This included several who had not previously struck me as having any particular interest in books; yet here they were, chatting away as if they were perfectly at home with authors and their work and had been all their lives.

For my own part, I felt no such assurance. I kept to the edge of the group. The ability to make casual conversation was what mattered. Most of the talk was not about writing. I did hear one of my classmates ask an author whether he typed his books or wrote in longhand. The author said that he always wrote on yellow legal pads with a no. 3 lead pencil, to which the student commented that Booth Tarkington said he used Dixon Ticonderoga pencils. I wondered how that particular student, of all people, could have known who Booth Tarkington was, much less that he wrote with a lead pencil. Later on I remembered seeing an advertisement on the inside back cover of the *Saturday Evening Post* showing Booth Tarkington at work, together with a statement of his reliance upon Dixon Ticonderoga pencils.

There seemed to be an offhand quality to the way that several of the authors talked, as if they were aware that they were on display and were making an effort to sound properly sociable. Most, however, appeared to be enjoying themselves and quite content to be Charleston Authors on parade, as it were. If I were an author, I thought, that would definitely not be my idea of fun.

As soon as felt that I could get away with leaving without appearing to be deserting the scene, I made my way out of the library. Outside in the hallway I encountered the faculty adviser of the school newspaper, who was chatting with another teacher and who may well have suspected what I was doing. "Taking off?" he asked.

"Yes, sir."

"See you in class," he told me, and added: "A lot of hot air in there this afternoon."

So the afternoon with the authors turned out to be quite other than what I had hoped it might be. I had thought that the authors of books would somehow be different from other people, although in just what ways I could not have said. I had assumed that the same thoughtful, informative, interesting personalities who wrote the books that I had read would be present and available in person. They would be full of information and literary talk about the craft of writing and, being Charleston Authors, they would hold forth on the literary uses of the local scene, both historical and present-day.

At least one of the Charleston Authors had indeed held forth at some length—but not about the craft of writing. Most of what he had to say was in the nature of complaint over the crassness of modern-day politicians and the wasteful iniquities of the New Deal administration in Washington. He also had things to say about the exploitation of the southern scene by certain fiction writers in order to curry favor and profit among northern audiences. Otherwise he talked about ancestors.

Not all those present had been as garrulous. What they had done was to stand in place, nod and smile, sip their tea, and be Charleston Authors. A couple of them, it was true, seemed uneasy at being there. Why then had they accepted the invitation to attend? I was not sure.

I thought about how some of my schoolmates had seemed to thrive at the event. They had chatted with the guests as if they were accustomed to the company of the authors of books from infancy on. When I thought about it, these were almost all boys I had first known when I had attended Crafts School in Downtown Charleston, before my family had moved back Uptown. Most of them lived in the historical section of town, below Broad Street, as did the authors at the reception. It may have been that as neighbors those students knew the authors personally. Yet that did not seem a sufficient explanation for their conversational fluency. If the authors had known how to function at the reception, so too had my classmates.

WHAT I WAS IN FACT responding to, without realizing it, was my first exposure to literature as a social art. I could not have sorted out my emotions at the time, and certainly not have articulated them. The phenomenon would puzzle me for years to come.

Whatever the private motives, creative and otherwise, that might have prompted the authors at the reception to write their books, they had been invited to be present in the capacity of Charleston Authors. It was like a role in a play. Presumably those who came did wish to fulfill that role, or at least had no objections to appearing in it.

Not all the authors asked had accepted the invitation to be there. So there must be some Charleston authors who did not consider themselves to be Charleston Authors. Either that, or they did not care to play the role in public.

I was sixteen years old at the time that the reception took place. By then I had decided that, like two of my uncles, I would become a writer. Fanciful ambitions to become a major league baseball player notwithstanding, it was the only thing that I had ever been able to do reasonably well, and I knew it was what I wanted to do.

The more I thought about what I had witnessed, the more dissatisfied I became with it. I had seen certain writers engaged in playing a role. Likewise some of my classmates had been playing a role. It was the need for the performance that dismayed me, I had stood by, looked on, and been unable to take part. I had been a failure at my own role.

I was irked with myself, and not only because I had been too shy to speak up. It was because I had allowed the occasion to matter, and was continuing to do so. After all, what difference should it make to me? Surely my hopes of some day becoming a writer did not depend upon whether I had or had not said anything at a reception. If some of my schoolmates had appeared completely at ease, what was that to me?

I vowed that whatever kind of writer I might someday become, I would never allow myself to play a role in any similar event, in Charleston or otherwise. The whole thing had been vanity. There had been no point to it—and moreover not in a million years would I be able to enjoy that kind of occasion. Others might want to stand around and be admired, but not I.

It was not for me. I was not cut out for it. Oh vanity of vanities.

THUS THE "DO YOU KNOW Your Charleston?" program and its culminating social event. Whatever its impact may have been upon me either then or later, in terms of the aims of its sponsors, it served its purpose. When several months later the report of the South Carolina State Board of Education accreditation visit was released, among the items drawing praise from the inspecting team were the innovativeness of the English curriculum and the imaginative use being made of the community's cultural resources to enrich the educational curriculum.

8

A Sort of a Saga

The years between my eleventh and nineteenth birthdays, from about 1935 through most of 1942, are in my memory spherical in shape, bound in horsehide with red stitching, and imprinted "Goldsmith 97 League."

Fateful events were taking place in the world then, but the development that was of most immediate concern to me during the winter and spring of 1941–42 was not the attack on Pearl Harbor, but the collapse of the Barreled Sunlight Painters.

In those days I possessed a formidable imagination. Merely by applying it, I was able at the age of eighteen to transform myself from a first baseman, a position at which being able to hit a baseball was considered important, into being a pitcher, at which it was not supposed to matter. I made this change without having previously done any pitching whatever and moreover in the dead of winter when baseball wasn't even being played. I acquired a Rawlings Bill Doak glove, had a metal toeplate installed on my baseball spikes, and in my mind the transition was thereby complete.

On our neighborhood sandlot team I always played first base, but when we had added other players and moved up to the city Twilight League, it became evident to me even before the season began that I was in over my head. I could not hit the level of pitching we were now facing. So I rode the bench, occasionally playing outfield for a few innings.

Not until the following winter did it occur to me that I might be a pitcher. My reasoning went like this: I could throw a baseball with a certain amount of velocity, and, to a degree, make it curve. I was left-handed. So also were King Carl Hubbell and Lefty Grove. Q.E.D.: I was a pitcher. It did not trouble me that as a first baseman I had tended to be less than accurate in my throwing. Left-handed pitchers, after all, were renowned for their tendency toward wildness.

So for this and other reasons I felt reasonably sure that when the 1942 summer baseball season got under way, the manager of our team, the Barreled Sunlight Painters, would be able to find a place for me on the pitching staff. Among those reasons was that I was also the manager.

OUR TEAM WAS NAMED after a brand of house paint. Sponsors were not too easy to come by, and the Atlantic Paint Company, which was willing to put up money for the baseballs, bats, and catching equipment, wanted the team called that. So the Painters we became, even down to wearing paint caps when we played.

In neighborhood baseball we had called ourselves the Rose Garden Rebels and played games with such other teams as we could schedule. The move up to the Twilight League, in which adults as well as teenagers played, for the 1941 season was a momentous venture. In actuality only a few of us on the Rose Garden Rebels made the move. The major part of our lineup—including the pitchers, the first and second basemen and the shortstop, together with a few others picked up from various sources—was recruited from the neighborhood teams we had played against. We were the youngest team in the Twilight League.

The Barreled Sunlight Painters lost their opening game of the season, won their second, and thereafter lost all their remaining games, ending up in last place. We were not quite ready yet for the more demanding brand of baseball.

The 1942 season, however, was going to be different; we felt certain of that. At seventeen or eighteen, while remaining the youngest team, we would all be a year older. Our best players would be playing for the Charleston High School team during the spring. Several of the others had graduated from high school and gone to work, but most were still in school. As a sophomore at the College of Charleston, I was the only one in college.

The United States was at war, and the various teams in the league could expect to have players departing for the armed services. In the several months immediately following Pearl Harbor, however, nobody that I knew had been called up as yet. In truth, during those early months of 1942 I did not think of the war as importantly impinging upon my own doings. It was meant for older people.

Prior to the rise of defense spending in the late 1930s, there was not a great deal of money in Charleston—nor had there been since the unfortunate outcome of the Civil War. It was the outbreak of war in Europe in 1939 and the looming possibility of American involvement in it that began changing everything. The Charleston Navy Yard was soon the area's largest employee. The U.S. Army Ordnance Depot and the Port of Embarkation, shut down during the Depression years, were reopened; new military and naval facilities including an army hospital were developed; a steel mill and other industrial plants were built; and the long-moribund harbor became busy once again.

The widespread popularity of baseball in the early 1940s seemed to be an emblem of what was happening. Most of the spectators were Uptown, which is to say working class and lower- and middle-middle class in origins, attitudes, and interests. They now had money to spend, and there were few public recreational outlets and facilities. Golf, tennis, sailing were not for them. When a professional franchise in the Class B South Atlantic—Sally—Baseball League was moved to Charleston and renamed the Charleston Rebels, fans flocked to College Park for the home games, and the turnstiles spun merrily.

As for the sandlot and recreation league baseball in the city, the immediate benefit of the advent of the professional Rebels was the availability of partly used Goldsmith 97 League baseballs at prices well below the standard $1.25 retail cost of a top-quality baseball. Hit over the fence during pregame batting practice or during games at College Park and retrieved by boys in the neighborhood, they were hawked, depending upon their condition, at twenty-five cents and if in near-mint condition a half dollar. Soon even neighborhood teams possessed ample supplies, and taped-up baseballs virtually disappeared from use even in pickup games.

One might have thought that once the war began, because of Charleston's nearness to the Atlantic Ocean a ban would have been placed on playing games at night. All along the eastern seaboard the U-boats were torpedoing coastwise shipping, which could be spotted all too easily in silhouette against the nighttime glow of urban areas in the sky. Yet not for long months after the devastating losses of freighters and tankers off the East Coast commenced did the U.S. Navy begin convoying ships. What is more, for reasons that remain puzzling, to the best of my recollection no blackout of nonessential illumination was decreed other than along the beaches themselves. Throughout the summer of 1942, the professional baseball season continued without interruption under the floodlights at College Park.

AS A LATE TEENAGER, I lived a kind of double existence, with two separate groups of friends and acquaintances—those with whom I attended college and those with whom I played baseball. There was very little overlap. In patronage and allegiance, baseball in Charleston was mainly an Uptown sport, while the college, although municipally owned and with many of its students from Uptown families, was in spirit a Downtown institution. The distinction was only roughly geographical, but intricately tiered socially. There were some four hundred students, all of them white, and of these fully half were women. The majority were local residents living at home; the college was without dormitories.

There were fraternities and sororities, the principal functions of which seemed to be to decide who was to be invited to join them. It was not exactly a democratic system, even for whites only, but Charleston was not exactly a hotbed of egalitarian thought. On the other hand, except for those students who were actively involved in the fraternities and sororities—of whom I was not one and neither were most of my friends—it did not matter a great deal.

The only major intercollegiate sport in which the College of Charleston fielded teams was basketball. There were no athletic scholarships, no part-time sinecures for athletes, and no tempering of academic winds to keep them eligible. It was owing to the last circumstance that I was enabled to make my appearance in an athletic uniform.

First-year students did not compete in varsity intercollegiate sports in those years; there were separate freshman teams, which played separate schedules. In my first year, the freshman squad consisted of ten members, or enough to make up two five-men teams at practice scrimmages.

The college had a barbaric habit of posting the term grades for the entire student body alphabetically in the hallway of the administration building basement, for all to see and compare. When on the appointed morning in late January the grades went on display, the name of the freshman basketball team's star forward was accompanied by an array of F's and D's. Not only did this render him ineligible for further athletic competition, but he thereupon dropped out of school.

So that scrimmage games could continue to be held during practice, I was pressed into service and assigned a uniform. From then on, in games with other schools when the score was lopsidedly in favor of our opponents, which not uncommonly happened, I was sometimes sent in for several minutes at a time to relieve one of the tiring regular players.

My moment of athletic glory came during a game against the Charleston High School team. We were losing by at least twenty points, which in that day of low-scoring games was equivalent to fifty or sixty points nowadays. The small crowd of College of Charleston students in attendance was becoming restless, and as sometimes happened, a few of them, out of sheer boredom, began calling by name for me to be sent into the game.

Previously this had occurred on several previous occasions in the closing stages of lopsided games, always to my acute discomfort. It was not that I objected to the idea of being sent out into the game, as that I was embarrassed to have the coach being badgered on my account. All I could do was to hunch down on the bench and hope that the coach would ignore the calls.

This time, however, a full five minutes still remained to be played when the coach instructed me to enter the game in replacement for one of the starting players. I was informed which opposing player I was to guard, and the teams lined up at midcourt for a center jump. The ball went up; the centers leaped for it; and I went racing down the court toward the basket.

A moment later I felt a heavy thud against the back of my neck. I turned to find the basketball rolling off toward the sidelines. Apparently the center jump had ended up in the hands of one of my teammates, who had caught sight of me all alone en route down court, and heaved the ball to me.

That I would ever have gotten a clean break to the basket, much less that the ball would have been thrown to me if I did, had not occurred to me. The spectators in the gymnasium, not a few of them members of the freshman class like myself, were convulsed with laughter. What the final score of the game was, I do not remember. It was not close.

WHEN BASKETBALL SEASON came around again in my sophomore year, I knew better than to try out for the varsity. I contented myself with keeping the score book and reporting the games for the next afternoon's newspaper. As the winter of 1941–42 turned toward spring, baseball began to dominate my thoughts once again. As usual my schoolwork suffered accordingly. During classes I began illuminating the margins of my textbooks with drawings of ballplayers and jotting down possible lineups for the Barreled Sunlight Painters—with my name listed among the pitchers. I ceased to spend all my free afternoons at the gym, and began stopping in at Hampton Park playground on the way home.

What others may have thought about my plans to be a pitcher was unknown to me. Nobody said anything much about it. I was in no way discouraged thereby. After a few months of allowing my fancy to enlarge on the subject, the assumption that I was a pitcher became so habitual in my mind that, without ever having aimed a baseball in the direction of home plate during an actual game, I had made it a fact of my identity.

ON A SATURDAY AFTERNOON in April the first Barreled Sunlight Painters practice for the 1942 season was held, even though some of our players, including our pitchers, were on the high school team and could not take part until the high school season was done. I wrote a paragraph for the afternoon paper announcing that the practice would take place, and several new recent arrivals in the area read the notice and asked to try out for the team. At the same time, two of last year's players reported that they would be departing for the navy before the new season started.

One of the previous year's Twilight League teams had been disbanded, and several of its former members showed up unannounced for the Painters' practice. They were in their twenties, several years older than the group who had formed our team. Their team had won the league championship two years previously, and I was flattered that they would want to play with us. I realized that their presence would mean that several of last year's players might very likely have to switch to different positions, but it was not, I told myself, as if any of last season's starters would be dropped from the starting lineup.

While the practice was going on, I was approached by the manager of a team from across the Ashley River in St. Andrews Parish, who proposed that we play a practice game with them at their diamond the following weekend.

My first thought was that until the players on the high school team could take part, we would not have enough pitchers for a game. This was at once superseded by the thought that, if we were to play the game, I could make my pitching debut.

On the appointed Sunday afternoon we drove across the Ashley River Bridge to the St. Andrews High School diamond, arriving well before the game was scheduled to begin. By the time we began throwing to each other preparatory to taking fielding practice, I had worked myself into a state of high excitement. So much so that, when chasing after a wide throw, I failed to notice a barbed-wire fence nearby. The result was a gash along my left kneecap.

"That ought to be sewn up," someone said. One of the older players offered to drive me back across the river to the emergency room at Roper Hospital.

If I did that I might well not get back to the field in time to pitch. I asked him instead to take me to a drugstore, where I bought a roll of adhesive tape, gauze, and Mercurochrome. Back at the field I bandaged and taped up the wound, then prepared to begin pitching.

Within two innings my knee had tightened up so perceptibly that someone else had to take over for me. By the time the game was done I was almost stiff legged.

My debut as a pitcher had not exactly been a resounding success. I had given up a couple of hits and walked several batters. Several errors had been committed behind me. Still it was not as if I had been routed from the mound, I assured myself. Had it not been for the damaged knee preventing me from properly pushing off when I threw, things might have been different. Bandaged knee and all, I felt quite satisfied with myself. I was a pitcher. To this day the scar on my kneecap is faintly visible.

AT THAT JUNCTURE everything came apart. What I had failed to consider was what last year's players might think about adding the older players. A week after the practice game and my debut as a pitcher, I was informed that several now wanted to be released from their contracts in order to form their own team. They had become accustomed to playing together, and they did not want to be part of a team with so many older players on it.

Next the two players on the Painters who had been with me ever since we had first formed our neighborhood team likewise asked to be released so that they could join the new team. It was obvious that they felt awkward about abandoning me, but they did not want to be left behind on a team that, now that the others were gone, would be consist mostly of players in their midtwenties.

I HAD COMMITTED MYSELF to accepting the older players on the Barreled Sunlight Painters, and I could not very well renege on the invitation. I could find replacements for those who were leaving. There were other good players who were also looking for teams. Very well, I would get along without them. I had every right to be indignant.

All the same, I asked myself, did I really want to be manager of a team made up of older players, none of whom I knew well, and some that I scarcely knew at all?

Forming the Barreled Sunlight Painters had been a way of continuing in baseball after we had outgrown the neighborhood team. I had organized the team and found a sponsor and been manager for essentially the same reason that my teammates were leaving the Painters. It was so we could play together. Whether I was the manager or only a member of the team was not of first importance to me.

I thought it over for a couple of days then called and asked whether there might be a place for me on the new team that was being formed. "Sure, Scoop," I was assured. "We figured you'd be wanting to come along too."

I arranged to turn the Barreled Sunlight Painters—name, sponsor, equipment, personnel and all—over to the older players and rejoined my baseball companions.

IT WAS ESSENTIALLY THE SAME team that had finished in last place the year before. There were two major differences. We were all a year older, even if still the youngest team in the league, and I was no longer the manager. My own contribution consisted mainly of cheering from the bench. I did get in briefly to pitch in a couple of games, with indifferent results. On one occasion I was scheduled to be the starting pitcher in a practice game out at a local army hospital against an army team, so before the game I bought a package of Beechnut chewing tobacco and loaded up, just as I had seen pitchers on the professional Charleston Rebels do. Not long before it was time to commence warming up, I began to perspire, and then the ground beneath me began tilting. I made my way over to a place behind a grandstand and lay down. I did not pitch that day.

Not long after the l season ended, my family moved from Charleston to Richmond because of my father's health, and I transferred to the University of Richmond for my junior year of college. I was determined to go back to Charleston for the summer baseball season, and in June I did return. Not, however, to play baseball, but to board a bus for Fort Jackson, South Carolina, and induction into the army.

So for the summer of 1943, instead of baseball in Charleston there was basic infantry training in Alabama, at which I proved to be even less gifted than at pitching. As for my baseball teammates, they were soon scattered far and wide, and before the war was over were to be found at assorted locales from the southwest Pacific to the Hürtgen Forest. Afterward not everyone came back home to Charleston to live. Several did not come back at all.

In the late 1990s, having retired from teaching, I was at a bookstore in Columbia, South Carolina, signing books, when a wizened little man came up to me. "Scoop!" he declared, calling me by my long-ago baseball nickname. "This is Sparrow! Remember me?"

Remember him? I certainly did. He had been the second baseman of the Rose Garden Rebels, deriving his name from his height, or lack of it. So small had he been that it was all he could do to throw a baseball over to me at first base—and, when he did, there was no guarantee that I might not drop it. When we had made the jump to being the Barreled Sunlight Painters, Sparrow had not attempted to come along, having accepted his baseball limitations several years before I did my own.

We talked about old times, about those of our long-ago teammates we had seen recently. Sixty years had gone by since then, and the two of us had never been close friends, but we shared something that was precious. When young we used to play baseball together.

9

THE ST. ANTHONY CHORALE

When I went to Staunton to work on the newspaper there I had the feeling, which I never afterwards quite lost, that I was moving to a far-off place, remote and different from what I had known. It is quite possible that if I had first gone there in any other season than wintertime it might not have seemed that way. As it happened, when the bus from Lynchburg turned off the highway east of the mountains to begin its climb over the Blue Ridge, it was soon traveling along a steeply graded road with ice and snow everywhere about, and I had the sense that I was engaged in traversing a high wall, a barrier that shut off the Valley of Virginia from the rest of the world. But it was not only the mountains and the winter; I saw later that it was also the way that I was at the time.

I was twenty-three years old then, and this was a little more than a year after the war ended and I returned to finish college, gone to work as a reporter in suburban New Jersey, then come back to Virginia. I had gone for a job interview in Lynchburg, and from there I took the bus for an interview in Staunton—pronounced, I reminded myself so as to be sure not to make a mistake, as if it were spelled *Stanton*, with no *u* in it. Once the bus left the main highway and turned westward, the ascent was steady, and soon there came hairpin turns and sharp climbs. From the window I could look along the slopes of mountains and down ravines for long distances and see only snowy hillsides and snow-covered trees.

It was a gray day and the clouds were low and heavy, a grayish white against the sky, so that it was difficult at a distance to tell just where the horizon ended and the clouds began. I wondered whether the deserts of Africa were any more desolate in appearance. The bus was a long time making its way over the summit and descending the western slope of the mountains, and even after it reached the floor of the valley and turned toward Lexington and Staunton, there were mountains in sight east and west, and snow in every direction.

The impression of the city of Staunton that I took that day was that it was a raw windy place, somewhat as I imagined towns might be like in the Far West. The wind was blowing very sharply, and though by then it was no longer snowing, fine grains of powdered snow from the mounds heaped along the sidewalks were flying about in the air. The sky had cleared a little, so that there were patches of blue. The buildings and stores of the city seemed old, as if built before the turn of the century or earlier. I saw very few trees along the street. Everything appeared open and exposed to the wind from off the mountains.

The newspaper office, which I found without difficulty, was the kind of old wooden building that I thought of as belonging to Civil War times. It had a show window, just like a store, with the words *Staunton News Leader—Staunton Evening Leader* in black-and-gold script on the plate glass, and above the second story a false front with scrolled woodwork and cornices. By comparison with the newspaper that I had worked on in New Jersey, and with others of my acquaintance, it was a very small plant, with business office, newsroom, composing room, and pressroom all located on the ground floor.

Even so I accepted the job when the publisher offered it to me. I had not been told whether or not there would be an opening for me in Lynchburg as a reporter on the larger newspaper there. The job in Staunton was as city editor, with a fifty dollar weekly salary—twelve dollars more than I had been earning in New Jersey. To be made a city editor, after no more than six months of full-time newspaper work, was an elevation in status. True, there was only a single reporter on the staff, and the city editor also handled all the telegraph, local, and sports news, made up the pages, and even edited the church news. Nonetheless it could be considered a promotion, and after all that had happened I was in no condition of mind to pass up anything that might enhance my estimate of my own worth.

The Sunday before I left New Jersey for the South I had gone up to Newburgh, New York, to see my uncle. He was my father's second-oldest brother and originally from South Carolina too. He lived by himself in a hotel room and had a collection of phonograph records. He had begun his career as a newspaper reporter and now wrote plays. Each evening, after finishing the day's stint at the typewriter, he would play music on his phonograph for an hour. In particular he liked the symphonies of Johannes Brahms.

What we usually did when I went up to visit him was to talk and listen to music. He had never met my fiancée, and did not offer an opinion about whether the cancellation of our plans to be married was a good thing or not. He merely listened. Talking to him about what happened made me feel less panicky, even though I was unable to bring myself to speak of the humiliation I felt.

I made out as if the breaking of the engagement had been a mutual decision, but I think he suspected what had happened. When it was time for me to return to New Jersey, he rode the ferryboat with me across the river to Poughkeepsie, and we walked out along the station platform. As the train had pulled into the station and I was about to step aboard the coach, he said, "Don't worry, bud, it'll all come out in the wash."

AFTER I AGREED TO TAKE the job in Staunton I rode back to Richmond on the bus to collect my belongings. My parents were pleased. They had understood why I had given up my job in the North, but would have preferred that I moved directly from it to another. As for myself, I too had begun dreading the possibility that I might have to ask them for help. When I had gone up to work in New Jersey, I had felt that at last I was going to be earning my own living and otherwise becoming, for the first time in my life, a successful young man, practical and self-sufficient, able to make my own way. And for almost six months, despite my small salary, I had been able to convince myself that it was so—until my plans had collapsed and I had lost any reason for staying up there.

The next morning I departed for Staunton, not on the bus but riding on the train, in a comfortable coach with a reclining seat. I had lunch in the dining car. Up ahead the locomotive whistled musically for the crossings. As I watched the Piedmont Virginia countryside pass by the window, I thought that it was a considerable improvement over the previous train trip I had made, when I had come home from New Jersey to Richmond, where my parents had moved during the war. The train that night had been late in leaving Washington and then had been delayed for several hours because of a wreck on the line just south of Fredericksburg. I had to sit a long time at night in an old, overheated coach with uncomfortable, hard plush seats, trying to read but more often staring out into the darkness, thinking how I was going back to where I came from, and not even able to return there without trouble.

My hopes for success as a newspaper reporter in New Jersey and then, as I had confidently expected, in New York City itself were gone. So too the notion that I might be able to emulate my uncle and move from newspaper writing into plays or, as seemed more appropriate to my interests, poems and stories. Instead I was back in the South, far away from where plays were produced and books published, and I had accomplished nothing. It had been after three in the morning before the train finally arrived in Richmond, and I had taken a taxi home and then had to beat on the front door for a long time before my father at last heard me and came down to let me in. "Well," he had said.

But now, en route to Staunton—pronounced without the *u*, I kept reminding myself—the immediate future at least seemed no longer so uncertain, for I was riding aboard a fast train westward to the mountains, to be the city editor of a daily newspaper, however small.

In Staunton the place I found to stay was on the top floor of an old three-story house that had been divided up into rooms for rent. The room was large, with windows on two sides, a double bed, a desk, an easy chair, and a washbasin. Compared with the tiny room I had rented in New Jersey for the same price, it was far more satisfactory. It was located just at the eastern edge of the business district, a block south of the campus of a women's college, and about five blocks from the newspaper office, up a steep hill. The city of Staunton was very hilly and had considerably more trees along the streets than I had thought when I first saw it.

The snow had melted a little when I arrived to stay, but it was still along the sidewalks and on the lawns and the rooftops. The people at the newspaper said that we would be likely to get several more heavy snows, for it was only February and the weather did not customarily break until about the first week in March. However, in my new job the weather would be of comparatively little importance to me, for from the time I began work in the late afternoon until I left the office after one o'clock in the morning, almost the only time I ventured outside the office was when I went out to eat dinner.

I came to work at four o'clock in the afternoon, checked the night Associated Press budget to see what was expected over the Teletype that evening, learned from the woman who was the paper's only reporter what she would have in the way of local news, then began diagramming the front page and editing copy. As the evening's news from the outside world began arriving on the Teletype, I edited it up and wrote headlines. The Teletype copy was in all-capital letters, and it was necessary to mark the capital letters before being set on the Linotype.

About six o'clock I went out to dinner. On the way I usually stopped at a newsstand to buy a magazine or a paperback book to read at dinner. An hour later I was back at work, editing copy steadily. Sometimes I took news over the telephone from a correspondent, and sometimes the reporter had an evening city council meeting or another such late story, but usually everything was on hand by ten o'clock, except for breaking news on the AP Teletype. If I had a story to send out over the AP, I scheduled it on the wire, and when the bells rang to signal me to begin, I punched it out on the Teletype keyboard.

When most of the copy had been set into type and I had edited and placed headlines on all the news that was to go into the paper, I went into the composing room and saw to the page layout, making cuts and changing the type around to fit. There were only two or three pages of fresh type, which was all that the plant's Linotype machines could handle in an evening. Much of the type we carried was picked up from the afternoon paper, with the headlines reset into the morning paper's typographical style and the time references changed.

By midnight we were usually ready to pull a proof of the front page, and after I checked it over for errors I went to work editing up some of the assortment of copy that was mailed in by rural correspondents in outlying areas, which would be set into type early the next day. The edition came off the press about one o'clock in the morning, and I was free to leave once I had finished editing up all the correspondents' copy and a few filler stories.

Several blocks away, not far from the railroad station, there was an all-night restaurant, and when I finished work I went there for what in effect was my supper. Since I knew no one, I sat by myself at the counter, reading the paper or a magazine while I waited for my order to be filled. After eating I walked up the long hill to my room. By then it was close to two o'clock or even later, but I was far from feeling sleepy yet, so I read for a while and listened to the radio. Because of the altitude I could pick up stations in the Midwest much more clearly than those to the east or the south. From two to three in the morning I listened as I read to a classical music program on a Chicago station, called the *Starlight Concert*. By three o'clock I was usually sleepy enough to turn off my reading lamp and go to sleep.

THE TRUTH IS THAT DURING all this time, from the very night I came back to Richmond from the North, throughout the several weeks of job hunting and now in the first weeks of my new job, I was waiting for a letter. Exactly what its contents were to be I should have been unable to say, even though I wrote drafts of it to myself in my mind from time to time. It was from the girl to whom I had been engaged to be married, and what it was supposed to announce was that everything was not irrevocably over between us.

It was not that I did not possess all the proof to the contrary that should have been needed to convince me. During the weeks after I left New Jersey I had come to realize in retrospect that the breaking of the engagement had not been a sudden decision but planned out well in advance. I saw too that her parents, both of whom I had liked very much, had undoubtedly been in on the secret, and the three of them had plotted how and when it was to be done. In my naïveté I had failed to read signs that were being flashed at me. No doubt her parents, who I was sure liked me, had been chagrined at my inability to realize what was taking place. That thought of that was so humiliating that I could not bear to think about it.

Yet despite the fact that such realization was intermittently coming to me, I was managing to keep from dwelling upon it most of the time, shoving it back into the periphery of my consciousness by assuring myself that it did not matter, that one day soon the letter would arrive that would change everything. There need not be an outright confession of error and remorse, a plea to resume as before, to have the engagement ring returned to her, to plan the wedding. What would suffice was a letter which took up as if nothing had happened, implicitly assumed a continuing relationship, expressed pleasure and interest in my new job, even hinted perhaps of a desire to come for a visit sometime to see me in my new surroundings.

BECAUSE OF THE LATE hours I was now working, when I woke up in the morning it was seldom earlier than eleven o'clock. I went out to a restaurant to get my breakfast while others were eating lunch. Then I stopped in the newspaper office to see whether there was any mail for me. Afterwards there were three hours or so remaining before time to begin work. Usually I returned to my room, since there was no place else for me to go. I hoped that there would be mail, for then I could answer it. If not, usually I read until time to begin work. The city library was located near my room, and several days a week I stopped in there to find new books, usually taking three and four at a time to my room. What I liked most were archaeology and Civil War history. The library was housed in the former residence of Stonewall Jackson's cartographer, the famous Jed Hotchkiss, and there were many books about the war.

During my first few weeks in the new job I was busy learning what was involved in getting out the newspaper. Not even in the afternoon, in my room, did I often think to feel bored or lonely. My first Sunday in town, when there was no paper to get out that evening, I had felt the time hanging heavy for a little while, but I wrote letters. I rather liked being there by myself in my room, listening to the New York Philharmonic concert on the radio, with the snow falling steadily beyond the windowpane. I could hear the truck traffic on the Valley Pike, which ran just below my window, laboring up the hill, and the road maintenance crews scraping the snow and spreading sand and salt on the icy grade. Later on, the westbound Chesapeake and Ohio train came whistling its way through town.

After dinner I wrote a letter to my uncle. He had responded to my account of my new job with the observation that it would be good training, though his guess was that after a time I might find a routine of desk work tiresome. I told him that while he might well be right, for now at least I found the editing quite interesting. I did not add that what I liked most of all was just that routine, and that the more hours a day it demanded of me, the more grateful I was for it.

THE DAY WHEN THE LETTER arrived was at the very end of February. It came in response to one that I had finally written, on a pretext having to do with the return of a book I had borrowed from a library some time ago and left behind me in New Jersey. It was one of the several letters waiting in my mailbox at the office, and my first, reflexive response was to shove it quickly to the bottom of the stack of envelopes I was holding, as if by postponing the reading of it, even for a few minutes, I might also postpone its meaning as well. For at that instant I was quite certain of what it would say, and I realized too that I had known all along. After a moment I tore open the envelope and hastily scanned the words, written in the familiar penmanship, on a double sheet of notepaper.

What was said was little more than a repetition of what had been said to my face a month earlier, together with the comment that my own letter had seemed to be written in anger and that she was happy to see that I was indeed angry, which, she said, I had every right to be. "The little bitch!" I said aloud, and looked around to assure myself that no one had heard me speak. "The little bitch," I repeated under my breath. For not only had I not written in anger, but I saw that by pretending that I had been angry she was assuaging any feelings of guilt she might have had at having hurt me. What I had accomplished by writing was to provide her with an opportunity to enjoy feeling distressed at having to decline my love.

I thrust the letter into my pocket and left the office. "The damn spoiled little bitch!" I said aloud as I walked up Coalter Street, after first looking to see that no one was within hearing distance. "Now I really *am* mad. Mad as hell!"

Yet as I was saying these things, I knew I was deceiving myself not at all. The truth was that I should have liked to be angry, to resent the way I had been put aside, as someone might put aside a novel when one finished enjoying it, or, more appropriately, I thought, as a child might put aside a set of finger paints once the novelty of being able to make pretty configurations with one's fingers had worn off. But I could not make myself feel anger—only a sense of humiliation.

I felt grateful that the barrier of the mountains existed, protecting me from further involvement. The condition to which I should aspire, I felt, was an emotional and moral numbness, a complete freezing of emotional attitude, of unconcern and indifference to my present circumstance, so that ultimately I might be able to bring my memory to a similar invulnerability.

And for a while it seemed to be working. I found that if I went to the office a little earlier than usual, and if I worked a little later after the paper had gone to press, I could stretch my working hours so that they filled most of my waking day, leaving only a brief period between the time I arose in the very late morning and went out to get breakfast, and the time I began the night's work, when my thoughts were not occupied by the requirements of my job. And after I had put the paper to bed and gone by for a sandwich at the all-night restaurant, I was sufficiently tired so that when I went to my room I could read about the Civil War or the exploration of the Upper Nile and listen to music on the radio until almost dawn without feeling restless or lonely.

After a few days I came to know something close to actual contentment at the way I was managing. I even decided that there would be no need for me to go home to Richmond on weekends. I would simply stay in my room and read. For the first time since I had come back South, I felt that I was close to being master of my emotions. I did not require anyone else's company.

HOW LONG I MIGHT have continued in this way if the winter had held on, I cannot say. But there came a day when the ice and snow were gone, the streets and lawns were wet from the melting, and the temperature was suddenly up in the sixties. Almost overnight the valley changed from a stronghold of frozen rock into a swiftly thawing garden. Everything around me now began turning toward color and warmth.

To the west of my room, and visible from my window, was a low mountain called Sally Grey, which had loomed over the little city in barren woods and stark granite. So perfectly had it seemed to match the frame of mind to which I aspired that I would sit and look at it for long intervals, as if through focusing my thoughts upon it I might acquire its hardness.

But now the bare crest was giving way to a faint but unmistakable green, and the trees along the slopes, which had seemed so sterile and rigid, were fringing into the blurred growth that softened and obscured the harsh outlines of the hillside. And late at night, when I finished my work and went by the all-night restaurant, I discovered to my dismay that the darkness, which until then had seemed so chilled and barren that I was glad to retreat to my room where I could read and listen to music, had now acquired a depth and resonance that I found threatening to my feeling of immunity.

Yet the night proved to be as much my ally as my enemy. For it was, after all, very late when I finished at the newspaper and had eaten my supper. I had been at work for ten hours and more, so that I was not obligated to reflect that under more fortunate circumstances I might have had the company of a girl—if I had a girl. Instead, by the time I was done with work, it was an hour when I could only have expected to be alone anyway, so that I did not need to be ashamed at my solitary condition or believe that if only I were more attractive and desirable than I was I would not be left to myself.

THUS ON A SATURDAY NIGHT in early April, after the paper had been printed and I had stopped by the restaurant, I found the night so warm and inviting that, instead of proceeding home to my room, I decided to walk down to the railroad station two blocks away. It was, after all, no longer Saturday night at all but very early Sunday morning, so that I need not feel, as I had so often done, that there was something wrong because I did not have a date.

The station was deserted except for a clerk in the ticket office of the lighted but unoccupied waiting room. I walked out along the platform to the west of the station, where the rock cliff that lay just beyond the double track slanted off. To the west I could hear a train whistle blowing, just as when a child I could hear the Seaboard freight blowing for grade crossings out in the darkness to the west of Charleston across the Ashley River. I would wait to watch it come through town before I went back to my room. I took up a seat on an empty baggage cart. Except for the whistle of the train, the city was still; I could hear an occasional automobile go by along Beverley Street three blocks away, but that was all.

Listening to the train drawing nearer, until eventually I could begin to hear the iron wheels reverberating along the rails, I felt a note of satisfaction in my solitariness that made the night seem not merely amiable but even harmonious, as if I were a part of it. To be seated there by myself in the darkness, past two in the morning, with no one else nearby and very few of the inhabitants of the community that lay around me still awake, seemed entirely appropriate. I felt a measure of pride in my separateness, a sense of resolution in being as I was, alone in the nighttime in a mountain town where I knew almost nobody.

The road that had brought me there, I thought, had been deceptive and erratic. It had not been remotely what I had imagined or intended for myself. Yet here I was, on a faintly warm night in the very early spring, with the city asleep around me and the C & O freight train blowing for the crossings as it neared town.

At length the train came banging into the city, the locomotive headlight probing through the darkness like a baton, until as it drew close the light thrust into view, in swift sequence, objects I had not hitherto made out: a row of boxcars on a siding, semaphores, telegraph poles, switch blocks, a warehouse alongside the tracks. It played upon the jagged rock wall of the cliff side across the way, breaking it into a mosaic of planes and recesses.

The locomotives—there were two of them, their drive wheels performing in unison—rolled powerfully up and past, and I could see for a moment the firemen and engineers in their cabs, high above the tracks, illuminated by the red glow of the open firebox doors. Then a boxcar, and another, and another clanged past, one after the other, chains rattling and the flanged wheels singing as they cruised along, their song punctuated with a chorus of creaks and bangs and bumps as the cars held to the rails, in cadenced processional, a hundred cars and more, until at last the sound lightened and the caboose swung past.

As I turned to watch it go I saw a trainman standing on the rear platform, lantern in hand, with the red and green lamps above him. He waved to me and I waved back, and I watched as the caboose receded rapidly past the columns of the station platform and into the darkness, the signal lamps solemnly glowing, and then around the bend of the rock cliff and out of sight. And all I could hear was the movement of the wheels in the distance, growing fainter as the train cleared the city limits and headed eastward. Further and further away, off to the east, the whistle sounded ever more distantly for the crossings. I sat on in the darkness, all by myself again, in no hurry to leave, listening pleasantly.

"The sleeping city," I said to myself, half aloud. I might write a poem entitled that. And only myself awake to listen. Lyrical whistle of the freight train, miles to the east and receding eastward. But then I heard another and, as it seemed, answering whistle, dirgelike and much fainter. The freight train could not possibly have moved so far away so rapidly. It must be the westbound passenger train, which came through the city each morning at about three o'clock. I looked at my watch in the darkness. It was indeed after three. If I waited for the passenger train to come and go, it would be almost four before I got back to my room and to bed.

And what of that? What was to hinder my staying here for as long as I wished, till broad daylight if I chose? Tomorrow I could sleep even later than usual. Besides, tomorrow was Sunday—more properly, it had now been Sunday for more than three hours. I might do whatever I wanted; there was no one to object. Because I worked when others slept, the night was fairly my own.

I could now hear two trains whistling; there was no doubt of it. They were both far away, but one was coming toward Staunton. There was a noise behind me, not far from where I sat. A man was engaged in loading some sacks of outbound mail onto a cart. When done he began pulling it up the concrete station platform. The train whistle was closer now, and presently I could hear the monotone of the wheels on the rails. Far down the platform, almost beyond the station, a man and a woman were standing, with suitcases alongside. That was where the Pullmans would be stopping.

Now the passenger train came gliding into the station, the headlamp abruptly materializing from around the rocky bend. The locomotive moved up and past me, immense and stern, its high drive wheels performing their revolutions very slowly. It pulled to a stop a hundred yards ahead. Opposite me on the rails was a darkened coach. I watched down the track as the porters swung down with their yellow footstools. Even at that hour there were some passengers debarking. The man and woman I had seen waiting now stepped aboard, with the Pullman porter following them, carrying their luggage; the arriving travelers walked off toward the station.

The train did not stay long. After only a few minutes I heard the conductor calling "All aboard!" and saw him signaling with his flashlight to the engineer up ahead. The air brakes went off with a hot iron hiss. The locomotive coughed twice in staccato explosion, and the train began easing forward into a slow, sustained rolling. I watched as the day coaches went by, then the dining car, cold and dark and the windows fogged, each to a swifter rhythm than its predecessor. Then the Pullmans: City of Ashland, Collis P. Huntington, Balcony Falls, Gauley Bridge. The last Pullman swept past in clattering haste.

The vestibule lamps receded westward. I listened until they were well out of sight. Soon the locomotive was blowing for grade crossings to the west of town. It would not be long before the train would have cleared the valley and begun climbing into the Alleghenies. As for the eastbound freight train, it was out of earshot now, and doubtless rolling along the grades of the Blue Ridge, bound for Charlottesville and the Northeast.

I walked to my room in the dark, feeling tired now and quite pleased with myself. It was well on toward four o'clock in the morning, I had seen two trains arrive and depart, and now I was all alone again on the deserted streets. I felt that I had accomplished something, had asserted my sensibility. I was persuaded too that whatever my present inconsequence, I was inevitable. On what grounds this assurance was to be based, and for what, I could not have said. Yet the certainty, as I thought of it, made me walk faster and breathe hard as I climbed up the hill toward my rented room, all by myself, at four in the morning, acting out a silent melodrama of prideful fulfillment.

THE NEXT DAY, HOWEVER, after I had gone out almost at noon to eat breakfast at the hotel restaurant, I felt no such assurance. My confidence, my optimism of the evening before, now seemed not merely misplaced but absurd. For in the light of a warmish Sunday in mid-April I saw myself in a different perspective, as a self-important young man with neither talent nor assurance, who had thus far failed at everything he had ever undertaken to do. I worked at a nighttime job that made it almost impossible to meet other people and to make friends and have dates with girls. And what was worse, I had been glad of it, because it enabled me to hide from myself the knowledge of my ineptitude and unattractiveness. Now, because it was Sunday and I possessed no such refuge for the ten or twelve hours before I could fall asleep again, I felt trapped.

I remembered how, the previous evening when the freight train had been calling in the night as if to me alone, I had fancied that I was going to write a poem about the sleeping city. What vanity! For I knew very well that on all occasions when I had attempted to write anything, I had been quite unable to produce three lines that were not empty, pompous, and flat. Whenever I actually sat down before my typewriter and tried to begin anything other than a routine newspaper article, all my confidence, and all the ideas I had in mind, swiftly went stale.

I read the Sunday *New York Times* in my room, then tried reading a book for a while, but could not escape my gloom. I decided to go out for a walk. Perhaps the spring weather would divert me. On Sundays there was an eastbound local passenger train that came through town about two o'clock. I would go down to the station and watch it.

As I walked westward on Beverley Street I saw several couples, my age or younger, strolling along, looking at the displays in the store windows, chatting happily. There were two couples who were holding hands.

Students from the local women's college and their dates, I decided. A year ago and I had might have been doing that.

I passed the Stonewall Jackson Hotel. Would I end up like my uncle, living in a hotel room somewhere? He didn't seem to mind. I envied him his spartan invulnerability, his hermitlike ability to live by himself and not care about anything except his work.

At the depot, waiting near the tracks, were a young man and several girls who seemed to be a little older than college age; they did not look like students. I walked past them, near enough to be able to hear what they were saying. They were talking with each other in French, and laughing at each other's pronunciation. They must be teachers at the college, I thought.

I should have liked very much to get to know people like that. I would have delighted in using my French as they were doing. But I had no excuse for venturing into their conversation. As if waiting for a train, I stood not too far distant, observing them from the corner of my eye. If only I had some reason, some plausible excuse, for joining them. Someone more sure of himself, more sophisticated and less self-conscious, would doubtless need no occasion, but simply go up to where they waited and strike up a conversation.

The train came drifting into the station. I had been so preoccupied that I had paid it no heed. One of the girls was apparently going away on a trip, or else returning somewhere after a visit to the others; the man was carrying her suitcase. I watched them as they said good-bye. Then after the girl who was leaving had gone inside the coach and found a seat by a window overlooking the platform, they were waving. "*Bon-voy-yage!*" one of the girls on the platform kept calling, mouthing her words very deliberately so that her friend on the train might read her lips.

If I were to go aboard, I thought, I might take the seat next to the girl and strike up a conversation. And why not? I might ride as far as Charlottesville and then take the evening train back to Staunton. I was free; I had nothing to prevent me from getting aboard and going along on the journey eastward. The thought frightened me, and instead I merely looked on as the railroad conductor signaled to the engineer, the vestibule doors slammed shut, the air brakes went off, and the train moved from the station.

The young man and the two remaining girls who had escorted the traveler to the station waved good-bye, then walked off toward the town. As they went by, one of the girls glanced at me for an instant. Hastily I averted my eyes, and so as not to seem to be following them, I walked a block eastward along the station platform and then took a side street back toward my rented room.

When I reached my room I turned on the radio. The New York Philharmonic Sunday concert was just beginning. Dimitri Mitropoulos was conducting the *Symphonie Pathetique,* which I disliked. Yet I did not switch it off. As if to punish myself, to make my afternoon complete, I lay on my bed, face downward, and listened to the oh so melancholy music.

They had been conversing in French. How very cultured, how very toney! And I, eavesdropping, watching them from a few yards away, had been standing there like a gawky fool and wanting to join them. The sensitive soul indeed. How very romantic! The lonely young man in the mountains! The thought of my pathetic posturing made me wince.

A few months ago on a Sunday afternoon, her father and I would probably have been playing chess and listening to this self-same concert. That *he* had been in on the plan! I writhed at the thought. During all that time, for at least a month and probably two or three, she had her mind made up to send me packing and had only been awaiting the "Proper Moment." But in my invincible vanity, I had proved so obtuse as not to see what should have been plain. So there had been the need to make it obvious, overt. And in discussing it, they had pitied me! The poor, naive young man from down South.

"Damn!" I said aloud, over the melancholy music. "Damn!" Who in the hell was she, who were they, to pity me?

It was true. Who *were* they? For while it was undeniable that I was lonely and missed very much having a girl, it need not be *her.* I could see that now.

I leaped up from the bed and walked across the room to the east window. The Sunday afternoon traffic was moving along Route 11. By God, I thought, I will write her a letter and tell her exactly what I think of her spoiled, stinking self. I went over to my typewriter, placed a sheet of paper in the machine. I stared at it a minute, then ripped it out. Hold on now, I told myself; just because you can see daylight you are not out of the woods just yet. It would be exactly what she would want—another sequel to the little game of "Falling Out of Love." I had had all I wanted of games. I crumpled the sheet of paper into a ball, threw it across the room at the wastepaper basket. It hit the wall, bounced in.

It must have been the people at the train station. I thought of how I should enjoy cramming their French conversation and their silly chatter down their cultivated throats. But that was not what I was angry about, was it? No, I had wanted to join them. My anger was for myself. Yet how could I expect to be other than what I was?

I lay in bed, and gradually became aware that the *Symphonie Pathetique* was concluded, and the commentator, Deems Taylor, was talking about the next number to be played by the orchestra. His mellifluous, too urbane voice droned on. Johannes Brahms had long put off writing a fully symphonic work, and it was not until he was forty-three years old that he completed his first symphony. The *Variations on a Theme by Haydn,* though originally composed for two pianos, was really a trial run, so to speak, whereby Brahms for the first time had used the full resources of an orchestra to develop an extended symphonic creation. The theme he had chosen, said Deems Taylor, was a choral work by Haydn, the *St. Anthony Chorale.*

Then, without warning, all unprepared as I was to meet it, there came the most cadenced, masterfully gentle music, calm and reassuring, that I had ever heard. In unhurried progression, tranquil and controlled, yet by no means without strength or resonance, the theme spoke out confidently, sustained and borne along by horns and violins. I had always liked Brahms, but this composition possessed a sweetness and harmoniousness that seemed to soften and transform everything around me—the air, the room, the time of day.

The music formed itself into an assertion, an acknowledgment of purpose, but without either panic or desperation. It climbed steadily forward, building to a more urgent reiteration, but only enough to make its point, without any clamor or abandonment of its dignity and congruence. It closed on three drawn-out, unhurried chords. ST. ANTHONY, I thought, as if punching out the letters on a Teletype keyboard. STANTON. Without the *you* in it.

The variations that Johannes Brahms had made on the theme by Haydn continued, and I listened on. But because I was young and had almost until that moment been in love, as I lay on my bed and the music played I did not think to wonder why it was that the pleasure I drew from the music was so like that which I took from the trains. Neither did it occur to me, being neither traveler nor musician but only a newspaperman temporarily resident in a mountain town in Virginia, to consider the odd coincidence in names, or even to ask who St. Anthony was. That truth, if such it proved to be, would come. For now, for Sunday afternoon, I was content to lie and listen to the music.

EPILOGUE

The Route of the Boll Weevil

> Every now and then, while our little train stopped at one or another
> of the halts on the Balbec line, I was struck by the strangeness of
> their names—Incarville, Marcouville, Doville, Pont-à-Coulevre,
> Arambouville, Saint-Mars-le-Vieux, Hermonville, Maineville;
> whereas, had I read them in a book, I would have been struck by
> their obvious points of similarity with the names of certain places
> in the neighborhood of Combray.
>
> Marcel Proust, *In Search of Lost Time*

The thought of traveling down to Charleston on the Boll Weevil had
crossed my mind before, but until then it had been scarcely more than a
pleasant fancy. That summer, however, the idea came to me that this might
be the chance to do it. I checked a Seaboard Air Line timetable, and trains
no. 25 and 26 were still listed as running daily between Hamlet and Savannah via Charleston.

Close to a decade had gone by since I had last seen the little gas-electric
combine and coach alongside the pink stucco station near the ballpark.
Throughout my childhood and youth, it was there waiting, seemingly forever, before resuming its run, an icon of summer and adolescence. I had
always wanted to take a trip aboard it. Once, during the war, I thought I
spied it on a siding when the train I was traveling on between Fort Benning
and Richmond while on furlough from the army, stopped in Hamlet,
North Carolina. But it was late at night, my train soon resumed its journey,
and I could not be sure.

I was living in Baltimore now, teaching at Johns Hopkins, and when the
summer term ended I planned to visit my aunts and uncles in Charleston.

I had visited Charleston a half-dozen times since we had moved to Richmond early in the war but always via the Atlantic Coast Line, a trip of just over seven hours. To do so on the Boll Weevil, I would have to take a train from Richmond to Hamlet, stay overnight at the railroad hotel across from the station, and board the Boll Weevil the next morning. According to the timetable the trip from Hamlet to Charleston took six hours—if the Boll Weevil made the run on time, which according to my recollections it frequently did not.

No matter. I would see all the little towns and hamlets whose names I used to read and wonder about. When a teenager I had a copy of the orange-covered Seaboard Air Line timetable, listing the places where the Boll Weevil stopped after it left Charleston for Hamlet: Yeaman's Hall and Inness and Cordesville and Witherby and Bethera and Oceda and Warsaw and Hemingway and Johnsonville and Eulonia and Centenary and Koonce and Halavon and Clio and Green Pond. And Hamlet itself; what an odd name for a town to have. Why, they might even have named it Elsinore. Was there a cliff there that beetled o'er its base toward the sea? Hardly—though far back in geological time the Sandhills region of the coastal plain had been the shore of the ocean. Now I would see what there was to see.

So in early July I rode down from Baltimore to my parents' home in Richmond, and on the following evening I climbed aboard the Seaboard Air Line's Silver Meteor, with its streamlined all-steel coaches and powerful diesel-electric locomotives.

It was 1:15 A.M. when the Meteor pulled into Hamlet. I walked down the platform toward the little hotel. In the lobby were the customary potted palms and somewhat frayed lounge chairs, the latter devoid of occupants at that hour. The Boll Weevil was scheduled to leave for Charleston at 9:45 A.M. I left a call for 8:30. My room was on the second floor and was without bath or running water. A large washbowl and pitcher were in place atop a bureau. An open window fronted on the brick wall of an adjacent building.

All night long there was the sound of trains. Hamlet was where the Seaboard line to Atlanta and Birmingham, on which I had traveled during my army days at Fort Benning, split off from the line to Florida. In addition to the Charleston-Savannah branch, another branch, between Wilmington and Charlotte, also crossed the main line at Hamlet.

Trains, diesel- and steam-powered both, both passenger and freight, clanged into town and through it. All of them passed by the passenger station and the hotel. Whistles sounded from far off, drew near; steam hissed, revolving locomotive bells tumbled, couplers clanked, chains rattled, boxcars clinked and jolted. Whenever a train moved through the intersection outside the hotel the crossing alarm bell began sounding. I wondered which of the numerous freight trains I heard had crossed the wooden trestle earlier that day over the Ashley River and moved through Charleston. Eventually I fell asleep.

In the morning the in-house telephone on the wall rang to awaken me. I ate breakfast at the hotel coffee shop, then, suitcase in hand, set out for the station. I walked along the long concrete platform. The Boll Weevil, with its gas-electric combination cab-engine-and-baggage compartment, was not yet in place.

The station was an unusual-looking two-story wooden structure with a wide painted dome that resembled a rain hat, and with overhanging roofs on both stories. Alongside were tracks with a small yellow-and-red diesel locomotive and a steam locomotive waiting at the heads of trains. I bought a ticket to Charleston, and asked when train no. 25 would be ready. "It's loading now," the agent said.

I went outside. "Where's the Charleston train?" I asked a nearby trainman.

He pointed toward the yellow-and-red diesel I had just seen. I had waited too long.

THE DIESEL LOCOMOTIVE was a Baldwin model, with a prominent horn protruding forward from the top of the cab like the barrel of a 37 mm anti-tank gun. Behind were a baggage car and a single day coach. The old steam locomotive that was wheezing and hissing across from it headed a somewhat longer train that would shortly be departing for Wilmington, 111 miles to the east.

I took a few photographs and went into the day coach, which was air-conditioned, with reclining blue seats, and divided into separate compartments for whites and blacks. There were only a couple of other passengers. I set my suitcase on an overhead rack, then stepped out onto the rear vestibule. Not far away was an unpaved street of white sand. So bright was the sunshine that it was difficult to tell which was the more dazzling, the reflection off the packed silica of the sand or the gleaming steel rails. Overhead the sky was clear blue. It was just as well that the coach was air-conditioned, which the Boll Weevil would not have been. It was going to be a very hot day.

A pickup truck was coming along the street toward the station, its tires kicking up white dust. Three men were standing next to the vestibule of a coach on the Wilmington train, conversing in low tones. Their bodies cast long shadows on the ground; it was still more than three hours before noon. The truck rattled by.

What I saw before me—the white sand street, the men conversing, the weeds growing alongside the tracks—appeared timeless, as if in place there forever. They were part of my experience, my heritage. I had not lived in the lower South for some years, was a teacher now at a university in the North. Yet I felt that I could walk over to where those three men were talking, enter into their conversation, understand every word they were saying, and why they were saying it.

Still, as I considered the matter some more, what I was seeing was *not* timeless. The train alongside which the men were standing and talking would soon be departing on its run to Wilmington, just as the train on which I was scheduled to ride would be making its way down into South Carolina and toward Charleston. In place of the familiar little gas-electric combine that I had expected to see, a diesel-electric locomotive was waiting to make the Charleston run. The steam locomotive on the Wilmington train was being phased out, not only on the Seaboard Air Line Railway but throughout the nation. The soldiers and sailors in uniform who had thronged the station platform in Hamlet when I had last seen it were no longer in evidence, for the war was over.

I went back into the day coach and sat down. As I watched, a black man, dressed in a suit and with a straw hat, walked along the aisle, through the section of the coach in which I was sitting, and into the separate, segregated section. My years in the North made that seem strange to me now, even a bit uncomfortable. There were other ways in which I was no longer as one in thought and expectation with those men who were conversing over by the vestibule of the Wilmington train.

Much that appeared unchanged was in fact changing all the time.

PRESENTLY THE CONDUCTOR outside called "*All aboard!*" and train no. 25, formerly but no longer the Boll Weevil, set out for Charleston and Savannah. It trundled across the main line in front of the station. The route led southward and southeastward down through eastern South Carolina to Andrews, about forty miles from the ocean, then turned southwest and paralleled the coast line through Charleston down to Savannah. We left the outskirts of Hamlet, moved through pinelands, past farms and fields. The conductor, a middle-aged man in a shiny black suit with gold buttons, collected my ticket. Noting my destination, he remarked, "Going all the way, eh?"

I nodded. "Is that unusual?"

"It is nowadays. Didn't used to be."

At Gibson, North Carolina, near the South Carolina state border, seven black men, four of them barefooted, were seated along the station platform, their legs dangling down in the sun. They were dressed in nondescript clothes and denim overalls, and wore caps of many colors. To a traveler from the North, they would be seen as local color quaintness. They probably did not have jobs.

At Clio, South Carolina, twenty-four miles down the line, there was a rickety Victorian mansion near the station, with unpainted corner towers, three-columned porch supports, tooled banisters, and frayed wooden shingles. On the back porch a rusty iron hand pump was mounted. The house may well have antedated the coming of the railroad; the chances of anyone having built a home like that next to the tracks, even before the automobile had made it both practical and fashionable to live on the outskirts of a town, seemed slight.

The conductor and several trainmen were seated in the coach talking, and I went over and sat down across from them. "What happened to the Boll Weevil?" I asked. "I was hoping to ride it."

It turned out that the gas-electrics had been gone for two years, replaced by small diesels that were especially designed for use on secondary passenger runs. Counterparts of the Boll Weevils were said to be still operating out of Savannah on the Seaboard's line to Montgomery, Alabama. The trainmen appeared to be in no way grieved at the Boll Weevils' departure from the Hamlet Division. The combines had often broken down on the job, necessitating repairs and putting them behind schedule.

I said that I had heard them called Boll Weevils ever since I was a child in Charleston in the late 1920s and early 1930s. "They used to call them 'doodlebugs' too," the conductor told me. The name "Boll Weevil" was unofficial, he said. The black people who lived in the Sea Island country along the coast came up with the name, following the advent of the bug that had wiped out the cultivation of long-fibered cotton during the 1910s and 1920s: "The bug was little, and the train was little, too." He quoted dialogue.

People said, "Where you goin?"
"Goin to Meggetts."
"How you goin to Meggetts?"
"Goin to ride the Boll Weevil."
"Oh."
They used to say, "That Boll Weevil, she run the fastest, stop the quickest, and stay the longest of any train."

It was obviously a routine he had delivered more than once, for the benefit of visitors who wondered about the name.

At Minturn, South Carolina, a girl in a faded pink dress stood at the doorway of a dilapidated tobacco warehouse. Inside were piles of yellow tobacco leaves. A red jeep bounced by on a sandy road. July was the season when the first tobacco crop was harvested and auctioned off at warehouses throughout this part of the Carolinas.

Another eight miles and we were at the edge of Dillon, where we crossed the Atlantic Coast Line main line. According to the Coast Line schedule, train no. 75, the Havana Special, would be passing through soon, bound for Florence and North Charleston. When I was growing up, it was always aboard the Havana Special that I had envisioned myself as one day leaving for the cities of the Northeast, and coming home as well. And I could have done so on this trip, traveling in style aboard a fast train with club car, diners, and a long string of coaches, pulled by three diesel units, leaving Richmond in the morning and arriving in the early afternoon, just as when a child I had watched it come rolling up to North Station behind a pair of steam locomotives. Instead here I was, riding along on the successor to the little Seaboard train, seeing places I had not seen before, and finding out at last where the Boll Weevil went.

After a few minutes the train came to a halt, and began backing along a wye into the Seaboard passenger station in Dillon. We pulled to a stop next to a covered platform. Beyond the rear vestibule of the coach, the tracks continued across what seemed to be the main street of Dillon, and on the far side and facing us was an old steam locomotive, its snout loaded with booster pumps and tanks. Behind the tender were some boxcars and a caboose. A way freight train, it had been working along the line ahead of us, the conductor told me, and had backed onto the wye to allow us and a northbound through freight to go by. The locomotive was suspiring lightly and a thin trail of coal smoke rose straight into the air. On its pilot, next to the main street, was half of a tiger watermelon, its innards partly consumed. A black flagman and white engineer were standing next to it talking.

I went down the vestibule steps and took some photographs. We stayed at the station almost fifteen minutes. I could hear the diesel locomotives and the train of boxcars of the northbound through freight drone through town a couple of blocks off to the west. Then our train began backing down along the wye and southbound onto the tracks.

We passed through Mullins and Gresham, then crossed a trestle over the Pee Dee River. The river water was black and the banks were tangled with bramble and reed grass. I had read somewhere that Stephen Foster had originally written his song as "Way down upon the Pee Dee River, far far away," but had thought better of it and substituted the more euphonious, if misspelled, Swanee. We moved through a succession of towns—Poston, Johnsonville, Hemingway, in country laced with swamps, creeks, and stands of cypress and oak. This was the country in which Francis Marion had operated against Cornwallis during the Revolutionary War:

> A moment in the British camp—
> A moment, and away
> Back through the pathless forest,
> Before the peep of day.

In the sixth grade in Charleston we had to memorize and recite it.

SO IT WENT. IT WAS AFTER 1:30 before we reached Andrews, a town of just under two thousand population. We were to be at the station for fifteen minutes, the conductor told me, and would wait until a bus arrived from Georgetown, down on the coast. Across the tracks was a swaying, unpainted building that the conductor said was a restaurant. The front porch slanted downward. On it were a swing and several chairs, one of them with upholstery half burned away by fire. Inside, on a plank floor, was a room with an oil heater in the center, several gray overstuffed chairs, and a sofa. Beyond was a long table covered with bright print oilcloth and red-and-chrome chairs arranged around it. A coffeemaker stood on a nearby wooden table with a stack of stoneware cups and saucers.

"All we got is ham," I was told by a woman who came in from the kitchen. I ordered a ham sandwich. It was packinghouse, not country cured, and was handed to me on a paper napkin. I took it back to the coach.

During the war, the conductor said, Andrews had been quite a busy place. A daily passenger train, not a bus, connected it with Georgetown, where there was a shipyard, and numerous people rode to Andrews aboard the Boll Weevil, then changed over to the Georgetown train. Andrews had been a railroad meal stop for years, he said, but not many railroad travelers patronized the restaurant anymore. I could well believe it.

The bus from Georgetown arrived, with two passengers on it. We set off down the line but soon pulled to a stop at Andrews Yard, where we moved onto a siding. We were to wait until a certain time for the northbound train, no. 26, then if it did not arrive, move on to the next stop and wait there. I went out onto the rear vestibule and down onto the ground. To the east of the tracks was a network of switching tracks, rusted and with weeds among the crossties and along the rails, and not a boxcar anywhere in sight. It was left over from the war, a brakeman standing nearby said; it had been crowded with freight cars in those days.

The anvil of a thunderhead was forming in the sky above a stand of pines to the southwest. We had left the Sandhills and upstate South Carolina and were in the lowcountry now, no more than twenty-five miles from the ocean. The afternoon air was hot, humid, and thick with insects. This time of year there was a thunderstorm almost every afternoon, the brakeman said. A thin young black man, he kicked between the tracks at the dried carcass of a snake. Off in the woods a bullfrog grunted.

The conductor, who had walked up to the locomotive, came ambling back. "Let's go," he said. So we climbed back into the coach and the train moved out onto the line, waited to pick up the brakeman, then resumed its journey. What happens, I asked the conductor, if the northbound train shows up on the line before we get to Oceda, the next stop? It won't, he said. The arrangement was that if it did not reach Oceda by a certain time, it was to take the siding when it got there and wait for the southbound section to arrive.

At Oceda several black people boarded the train. We waited at the siding. Presently no. 26 came into sight, moving at a brisk clip. It clicked past us, red-and-yellow diesel, baggage car, and single daycoach, and up the line, bound for Hamlet. We returned to the line and were off for Charleston.

The sky had grown darker, and soon the rain came, driving hard against the windows of the coach. I could see the lightning flashes, but the accompanying thunderclaps were faint, their sound masked by the air-conditioning and the running of the train. A few minutes more, and the rain slackened off; we had passed through the thunderstorm.

We were coming into the Santee River flood plain, with marshes and creeks and shaded recesses of woods draped with Spanish moss. No doubt there were alligators in the dark water and very likely black bear in the thickets and woods. The river itself was quite wide with a belt of marshland along the banks. Beyond it, on solid ground again, we passed through stretches of farmland with black soil, then more marshes and creeks and cypress trees with knobs. We could not be too far from the area called Hell Hole Swamp, which during Prohibition days was one of the prime centers of moonshine production on the south coast.

There were extensive tracts of open marsh grass and streams, with the tracks running above them along a wooden trestle. This was the upper reach of the Cooper River, which together with the Ashley formed Charleston Harbor. As often as I had gone down to the Charleston waterfront and watched the ships, tugs, trawlers, and small craft, the upper Cooper was unknown territory for me. Herons and egrets were in place along the brackish marsh; here and there were duck blinds camouflaged by reed grass. I could remember, as a child, paddling along the marsh creeks on the Ashley River in a leaky wooden boat. Clouds of tiny white insects might rise up when I rounded a bend, or an occasional startled heron or marsh hen that would fly up suddenly and wing away.

But now we were moving down onto the Charleston peninsula. When a child I used to wonder where the route of the Boll Weevil led after it left the pink stucco station at the ballpark. How did it make its way through

Charleston Neck and North Charleston? The path it took through the city had remained unknown to me.

Back then the little train had seemed so familiar, so ordinary, totally without surprise or mystery. Yet there were places that it went, areas it traversed that I did not know, even in Charleston itself.

We passed the U.S. Army Port of Embarkation, where in the first summer of the war I had a job as a checker, supervising a gang of workers unloading freight cars. Then we were in North Charleston, crossing the main street. I had worked there one summer as a reporter on a little weekly newspaper housed in a ramshackle old store, not a mile up the way.

Now we were rolling past the navy yard, where during my childhood my father would take us on Sundays sometimes to play aboard the wooden hull of Admiral Farragut's old flagship at Mobile Bay, the *Hartford*.

The twin arches of the Cooper River Bridge were in sight to the south, spanning the harbor. Then we were moving past Magnolia Crossing, past the cemetery, where my father's mother and father, whom I had never known, were buried, and out into the marshland and open areas along the river. Beyond the bridge as we drew nearer, I could see masts and funnels and gantry cranes. Then the tracks curved away to the westward, but before the train reentered the Uptown city I caught a quick glimpse of Downtown Charleston, and the harbor beyond. From where I watched now I could see them both, Downtown and Uptown, not as separate entities but as parts of one place, a city that I knew and loved.

So this, when seen inbound from the north instead of outbound as I had always assumed it would be, was where the Boll Weevil went! Of course it was changing! How otherwise could it remain itself?

TRAIN NO. 25 SLOWED to a crawl as it moved across the intersection at King Street and along Grove. The Rutledge Avenue crossing barriers came down, and the alarm bell clanged. The train passed by the grandstand at College Park and came to a stop at the stucco station.

I lifted my suitcase down from the overhead rack, stepped along the aisle into the vestibule and down onto the concrete walk alongside the track. I walked through the baseball parking lot over to Rutledge Avenue, crossed Grove Street, and waited for the bus.

An odd thing happened then. A boy came wheeling along the sidewalk on a bicycle, a baseball glove looped through the handlebars. I started to speak his name: "Billy!" Then I realized that this was a much younger boy who happened to resemble someone I had known ten years earlier, for the Billy I remembered would be a grown man in his middle twenties. The Rutledge Avenue bus came along, and I got aboard and headed downtown to my aunt's.

That was in July of 1950. A week later I went back to Baltimore on the Havana Special. In early September the college year began. That fall I met the girl who would become my wife.

Charleston native LOUIS D. RUBIN, JR., has been an author, an editor, a publisher, an artist, a newspaperman, and a university professor during his distinguished career. Rubin has served as chancellor of the Fellowship of Southern Writers, president of the Society for the Study of Southern Literature, and chairman of the American Literature Section of the Modern Language Association. Cofounder of Algonquin Books of Chapel Hill, he has written and edited more than fifty books, including most recently *The Summer the Archduke Died: Essays on Wars and Warriors*, *Where the Southern Cross the Yellow Dog: On Writers and Writing*, and *My Father's People: A Family of Southern Jews*. He and his wife, Eva Redfield Rubin, live near Pittsboro, North Carolina, not far from Chapel Hill. They have two children and two grandchildren.